Living 01

A Modern Cat—astrophe

Audrey June Chandler

Pen Press

First published in Great Britain by Pen Press

All paper used in the printing of this book has been made from wood
grown in managed, sustainable forests.

ISBN13: 978-1-907499-48-7

Printed and bound in the UK
Pen Press is an imprint of Indepenpress Publishing Limited
25 Eastern Place
Brighton
BN2 1GJ

A catalogue record of this book is available from
the British Library

Cover design by Jacqueline Abromeit

Don't read too much of the book – it'll have you in tears. The author, Audrey, is a lovely woman who took in, fed and loved, 35 feral cats in Spain.

"The cat has too much spirit to have no heart"

Ernest Menault

"Sometimes he sits at your feet looking into your face with an expression so gentle and caressing that the deep of his gaze startles you. Who can believe that there is no soul behind those luminous eyes."

Theophile Guatier

This book is for Carlo, Tanya and Zane.

Dedicated to all the cats that have told their story in this book.

To all the cats whose stories are written only in the hearts of the humans who shared their lives, and to all the cats whose stories will never be known.

Thank you to my Publisher for bringing this book to life.

Story One

Little House by the Sea

The sun was shining out of the big blue sky, casting sparkles on the turquoise sea as it lapped gently onto the shore of the sleepy little fishing village where I grew up. A few clusters of white-washed cottages hugged the edge of the shoreline and a small boat lay basking under the heat of the sun, its nets strewn out to dry after the lone old fisherman's morning catch. A group of seagulls perched on the sandy beach, resting before their next journey.

I sat on the steps to my home, cleaning myself in the warm sunshine. It was such a glorious morning and all I could think of was how lucky I was. My life was good, my world safe, and my destiny decided. I had seen to that. I knew how I wanted things to turn out for me, and I had taken the necessary path that would lead me to my dreams.

Of course this did not meet with my mother's approval, and many times she would chide me, but I knew that I did not want to be like her, endure the life she had lead. I loved her dearly, she was a good mother and I admired her strength and courage, but I could see the demise of

1

my family and the life that awaited me, should I follow in her footsteps. My mother had told me many stories of my family`s struggle for survival, and the many wars that had been waged for this part of the cove. Our colony had lived here for many years, and had a long line of social standing. This was our land, and our beach. She was our queen and my father was king.

I don't remember much about my grandmother, but I will always have a picture in my mind of the first time I saw her, on an evening of the full moon. Then, as she so often did, she had summoned the elders of the family to join her and there they sat, in silence, at the water's edge, as the moon sailed over the night sky. I never understood why, and when I questioned my mother on this, she told me, "When the time is right, my little princess, you will learn the secrets of our kind."

When I was very young, and I first became aware of myself, I knew that I was different from my siblings, even though we were identical in appearance, with the same fluffy pink noses and little white faces. They all seemed happy just to play, sleep and feed. But I wanted more. I wanted to learn more, and I wanted to know how I got here and where I was going. So I spent most of my growing days watching and listening to the old and new stories, and annoying most of the elders with my persistent questioning.

As I sat on the step that morning, feeling happy with my life, and having learned all that I had, I could not help the ache in my heart for my family and how they were living their lives. Their very existence was a daily struggle. Once part of a proud and strong colony, they were now reduced to little more than beggars that roamed the beach, searching for scraps of food.

Gone were the caves along the cliff's wild and rugged edge, where they had once lived. The new highway had seen to that. Gone was the old mill, which had stood crumbling for many years, giving them shelter. Gone were the thick bushes that grew along the sand's edge, offering a place for them to sleep. Modernisation and renovation had taken it all away. The only refuge left for my family was the storm drain, which jutted out onto the beach with wide and empty mouth. Or the hills over the new highway, which for now remained wild, but to get there, one had to take the suicide run. Gone were the many fishermen, who would take their boats out to sea, then return with plenty of fish for all. Now dinner was what the sea threw up after a storm, scraps left by the humans who spent the day at the seaside, or what the old fisherman's wife threw out over the cottage wall.

It was in these dark times of hardship, while my mother was heavy with child, that a dim ray of hope shone upon her life. Just as the last of the old thick bushes were being pulled out of the sand, and her last refuge taken, some humans moved into one of the little old cottages. Not being fond of the human kind, she blamed them for much of her family's downfall, and she kept her distance. To her they were a source of food, an opportunity for a meal, nothing more.

It was my older brother and twin sisters from the previous litter who made the first move. These humans had rescued one of my cousins, a little kitten they had found lying at the opening of the storm drain. He was very weak and possibly dying. I learned from my aunt that they were all on the verge of starvation, there was not enough food to go round, and while she was out on a hunt that day, his siblings forced him, being the weakest, out of their "cave". The humans took him into their home, nursed and fed him, and before long he was back on his feet. He was bathed and cleansed of any parasites, given his own bowl of food and put on the patio with a little basket and blanket.

Curiosity or hunger got the better of my brother, and it wasn't long before he crawled under the little wooden gate, followed a little hesitantly by my sisters. A close friendship developed between the four of them and soon they were inseparable. Although at first my aunt tried to

4

rescue my cousin from the humans, he would always go back to his new home. Having three other young to feed, she took the situation as a blessing, and gave herself to the task at hand. I learned later that while out on a rummage for food one night, two of her young had followed her over the highway, and subsequently lost their lives. The last of her litter was eaten by a pack of wild dogs that roamed the beach and hills.

The humans must have become aware of the plight of my family, because a bowl of food was placed on the steps just outside the little wooden gate every evening. Without them realising it, this gesture, although a kind one, was in fact the catalyst for a war.

With the onset of winter, and the many changes that had taken place in our little cove, food was the only key that could guarantee survival. The king from the colony on the other side of the cove had heard of the abundance of food in our land. Rumours began to grow about the feasts that were being bestowed upon us, and that we had more food than we could eat. In truth, it was only enough to feed a handful of my family, but these rumours had spread like a fire to dry grass. The king took it upon himself to confront my father, telling him that he wished to take our land, our queen and our food. My father faced the challenge and declared war upon the king if he tried.

And so it was, on a cold winter night, that the king my father went into battle. The screams and the raging pierced through the darkness like a slashing knife, and could be heard for miles around. My father fought the bloodiest battle of his life. He was older than his enemy, and not so sure-footed, but every time he fell, he would rise again. Clawing, ripping and biting. There was blood and fur flying into the air with every attack, as they rolled and twisted about on the sand. Neither would surrender, it was a fight to the death.

My mother, grandmother, elders and young ones all looked on in horror and fear. No one dared to think of the outcome, should my father lose this battle. It was at that moment, when the fight was at its most ferocious, that my mother closed her eyes and prayed. Victory could only belong to one of the kings.

Suddenly, in answer to her prayer, a bright beam of light shone out over the sand, and a human voice called from the little cottage gate. Within a blink of an eye, the humans were upon the two kings, waving sticks and shouting, trying to separate the mangled bodies. The enemy scurried off across the beach and disappeared over the rocks, vowing to return, and my father limped out into the night.

The battle was not over. It would be fought another day.

Everyone else had hidden from the humans until they had gone, and when all was quiet, my mother crept down to the scene of the battle. She sniffed the ground for my father's scent and, since he had lost a lot of blood, it was not difficult to follow the trail to where he was hiding. What she saw horrified her. His wounds were the worst she had seen in all her experience of war and its destruction. He had lost part of his ear, a claw was still clinging to the ripped lid of his eye, but worst of all his wounds was his tail, which had been completely stripped of skin, baring the flesh and bone, leaving the fur still scrunched up on the end. He lay trembling in pain.

Realising that her fate and the fate of our family was in jeopardy, and that my father would not be able to stand against his enemy, at least not until he recovered, she began to panic. With her belly swollen and her heart heavy, she licked my father's wounds and comforted him. As she lay beside him, her mind in turmoil, she devised a plan. When she told him of this, he tried to argue but was in no state to do so. "There is no other way!" she cried to him. "If we are to try to save our family and our land, and if I am to try and save you, my lord, then I must do what must be done." She told me that they both wept at the outcome of this life that was theirs.

A few days later, her plan began to unfold. Summoning all her courage, putting aside all her pride and pushing her distrust of humans into the very back of her mind, she climbed the steps to the gate of the little white cottage, walked along the wall and jumped down onto the patio. Desperation had brought her to this place; she had nowhere else to go. Nowhere that could possibly offer any safety or protection from the enemy king. The humans who lived in this place had shown kindness and compassion and, just maybe, they would understand.

It turned out to be the best decision she could have made, in the situation that faced her. The humans, seeing her swollen belly, allowed her to stay, and she was given a box in which to give birth. Two days later, I was born, along with my four sisters. My mother told me of how it had taken many hours to pass us from her body, and how the female human had stayed with her, stroking her and comforting her through all the pain. Never before had she allowed a human to touch her, and yet never before had she felt so safe. After the last of us were out into the world, she fell into a long and deep sleep, while we suckled on her breasts.

The first thought my mother had when she awoke was for my father. She had not seen him for several days, and was anxious to hear news of him, but she was too weak to walk. There was nothing that she could do, or so she thought. My elder brother, being the curious sort, sneaked into the room where the human had placed the birthing box. After sniffing it for a scent, he gently stood up, his front paws resting on the top of the box, and peered in cautiously. My mother was so relieved to see him and told him to go and find my father. "Tell him to come here, it is a safe place, and the humans might be able to attend to his wounds. Tell him that he has five new daughters and that I am fine."

The following morning my mother was woken by a scream of horror from the humans. With a feeling of panic, she found the strength to jump from the box, and run in the direction of the commotion. My father was stretched beneath the chair on the patio, all his wounds revealed in the bright daylight of the morning. The humans were obviously distressed at the sight of his mutilation. They tried to coax him into their care, but it was not them he had come to see. After several painful attempts, he managed to scramble over the wall and disappear back into the drain beside the cottage.

It was a while before anyone saw him again, but the humans began leaving food at the entrance to the drain, in the hope that it would give him the sustenance he would

9

need to recover from his wounds. Hope was all my mother could do. She knew that my father was too proud to submit to any of his enemies. She had hoped that, in time, he would change his mind. But for the moment, she needed to protect her family.

*

When my sisters and I were a few days older, between the feeding and nursing, my mother began to set the rest of her plan into action. She would scurry off to find the rest of the family, summoning them to the cottage. Slowly and with much caution, the family began to move onto the patio. My aunt came, carrying her newly born young in her mouth, having had to make several trips. All my cousins, my older brother and sisters obeyed the call. My mother had managed to gather all the family into the safety of this fortress held by humans. All except for my grandmother and of course my father. They were both too stubborn and strong in their beliefs, far too proud.

Lookouts were posted on the walls and roof to keep watch for the enemy, and an eye on the drain entrance, wherein my father lay. My mother knew that the enemy king would surely return, but not when. The young played in the confines of the walls, unaware of the imposing danger. The king had fallen and his land and subjects were in jeopardy.

All the while, my sisters and I stayed sleeping in our box, and the humans looked on in silent amazement.

One morning, the female human went out onto the patio, and as she opened the door, she jumped back in surprise. The king, my father, sat in the doorway, looking very dishevelled; he had lost a lot of weight and was riddled with infections. She went to touch him, but he drew back; then she went to fetch him a bowl of food, but he showed no interest. Not sure of what he wanted, the human stared at him and he stared back, as if both were waiting for something.

After a delayed moment, an idea sprang into her mind and she went to fetch the birthing box, wherein my sisters and I lay sleeping. She placed it on the floor of the doorway and stood back. My father crept gently up to the box and peered in. He sat there for a while, looking down at the bundles of breathing fur, then turned and walked away. He was never seen again, but the dried bone of his tail was found a few days later, under the wicker table.

Things stayed uneventful for some time. Everyone settled into their new surroundings, but always on guard. The enemy king had been seen in the distance, obviously noting the entire goings on, and trying to work out how to deal with the situation. This was a strategy that he had not seen before and it would take a lot of cunning to attempt an attack. With the humans offering protection to his enemy,

11

and not certain of my father's whereabouts, he knew that an attack was not going to be easy.

*

In the meantime, my sisters and I had grown adventurous, and began to leave our box in search of something more exciting than each other. We climbed anything that was climbable. Up the legs of chairs and tables, sinking our needle-sharp claws into sofas and beds, scrambling up curtains, and of course knocking any small objects crashing to the floor. It wasn't long before all five of us were moved out onto the patio to join the others. We had never seen the outside or even, in fact, anyone else. All we had known was my mother and the humans. We knew nothing about the war, and all that was going on.

At first, the bright sunshine blinded me, but once the shock passed, I found myself staring into a wall of eyes. I sat there, not sure of what to do, waiting for someone else to make a move. Then I noticed my mother, who had been sitting on the whitewashed wall, jump down and walk over to where my sisters and I had been sitting. She licked each of us in turn, and then called to everyone, "I would like to introduce to you the new additions to our family, my five lovely little princesses." To which, much to my annoyance, everyone came over and began making a fuss of us.

So, that was how I became part of this great family that lived on this side of the cove.

*

The patio was quite a large area, half shaded by a wooden pagoda, under which stood a blue painted wicker table and two matching chairs. There were several large planters bursting with colourful shrubs and plants of reds, oranges and yellows. Trellises, carrying their heavily laden vines, clung to the white surrounding walls. In the far corner, beside a large wood pile, stood a barbeque, the lower half of which had become a home for my aunt and her kittens. Some tall pampas grass grew in the sand, beside the gate where it met the front wall of the cottage patio.

Most of my days were spent with the young ones climbing the pagoda, or jumping off the wall into the pampas grass. The older members of the family spent most of their time sleeping on the wicker chairs, on the table, or on the sun loungers in the middle of the patio. Except, of course, those who sat on the wall, watching.

One day a few of the young ones grew bored and decided to continue their game on the pebble path leading down to the beach. I had not joined in, but had remained sitting on the step below the gate.

13

All of a sudden, as if out of nowhere, a huge black dog appeared from around the corner, barking like a crazed monster. He lunged at the others, sending them scurrying in all directions, to disappear into the undergrowth of the grass bush, or up the steps and under the gate. I just sat there, frozen, unable to move my legs. Trembling with fear, I stared into the wild, burning eyes of the mad dog as he bared all his teeth and gums, and I sensed that I was about to die.

Suddenly, a shadow touched my face as it passed, and within a timeless moment, my mother was between me and the cat-eating monster. Her back was arched, her fur on end, and her tail erect. Standing her ground, she hissed at the dog, daring him to move any closer. He began to bark even more ferociously, took a step back, and readied himself for the attack. But my mother kept her stance, showing not a flinch or flicker of fear. Something told me that it was no longer I who was about to die, and I finally managed to move my legs. I slid under the gate to the safety of the patio, leaving my mother to the mercy of the wild and raging dog monster.

My aunt and a few others sprang up onto the wall, looking down at the scene in horror. They too readied themselves for attack; one wrong move from the dog, and he would taste the blood that their sharp claws could draw.

The stand-off lasted several minutes, with the enemies glaring into each other's eyes. Even though my heart was pounding, it was filled with admiration for my mother's strength and bravery as she stood her ground.

Finally, she moved forward – only one step, but it was enough to unnerve the dog and he stepped back hesitantly, panting, his tongue hanging from the side of his mouth. The others then jumped off the wall and came up behind my mother. It must have been too much of a challenge for the dog, because he gave a whimper before turning and running away up the beach.

He wasn't the only one to learn a lesson that day. I learned to fear the wrath of my mother as she chided me for my foolishness. Not only was it a scary world out beyond the gate, but my mother was frightening too. I just wanted to go back to where I felt safe, and so I ran back into the house. The birthing box was no longer in its place so, looking for somewhere to hide, I jumped onto the humans' bed, dove between the pillows and crawled under the covers.

*

After that day, I never ventured from the confines of the house, and it wasn't long before the humans noticed me around; after all, I was the only one, besides my rescued cousin and older brother, who didn't shy away whenever

15

they were about. None of the others would let the humans touch them, and even my mother, who allowed an occasional stroke or two, showed signs of disdain. It seemed that they were either afraid or didn't like humans, and I couldn't understand the reason for it.

Having me around seemed to please one of the humans. She began to talk to me as if I was one of her kind, and I was given a name. "Hello, little Princess," she would say. "Do you want to come and sit on my lap?" Of course I would oblige, give a little meow, then jump up and nestle on her knees, always purring to show my appreciation of her affection. Sometimes she would just stroke me and other times she would tickle me playfully.

I knew that I had won her heart and secured my place in the house when she came home one day from a shopping trip with a gift for me. "Princess, come to Ma, I have something for you." I walked over to where she was sitting on the sofa, and jumped onto her lap. She opened a little bag and produced a pink collar with sparkly flecks and a tinkling gold bell. She fastened it to my neck saying, "You are now the prettiest little Princess in the world." Giving me a kiss and a hug, she set me down and wandered off into the kitchen, only to return with a new pink bowl, with the word "PRINCESS" written in gold on the side. She set the bowl on the floor, and inside were some of the smallest fish that I had ever seen.

While I tucked into the contents of my new bowl, Ma carried a much larger bowl of these fish outside on to the patio, to the meowing frenzy of my family. Then I heard her open the gate and walk down the steps. By the time she got back, I was licking my bowl clean. She walked into the house, calling for the other human."Danny, I think something has happened to Daddy cat, he hasn't eaten his food for three days now."

I had no idea who Daddy cat was, but whoever he was, the humans seemed to be quite concerned about him. They both went out of the gate, so I jumped on to the kitchen windowsill to see where they were going, the bell on my new collar tinkling. I looked out onto the patio and noticed that my mother was on the wall, peering over at the humans and the drain. The sound of my bell turned her attention to me, and for a brief moment our eyes met. I thought that I had seen a tear, but she looked away before I could be sure.

Later that afternoon I approached my mother on the subject. She was napping on the chair, under the shade of the pagoda.

"Mother?" I asked cautiously. "Who is Daddy cat?"

She shifted her position slightly, and replied with a note of hesitation in her voice. "He was your father."

The words rang in my ears. Had she just said that he was my father? That he *was*, and not *is*, my father? I was

17

about two months old, and had never even thought about him or even wondered if he existed. But then I'd never known him.

"What do you mean when you say that he *was*?" I asked.

My mother jumped down off the chair and came to sit beside me. "Your father passed away, only a few days ago."

"What do you mean by passed away?" I asked.

"Well, he has gone to a place where the spirits fly on silver wings in the sky."

"Will he come back?" I asked.

"No, my little one, he can never come back, but sometimes a little piece from his silver wings will fall from the sky, and if you catch it, you will have a part of him to hold forever."

A feeling of sadness came over me and I cried, "Why didn't I know him, why didn't he say goodbye?"

My mother comforted me with a lick on my cheek and replied, "He did say goodbye to you, my child, but you were asleep."

I sat there for a while, feeling like I had lost something very important, and then: "Tell me about my father, please?" I begged.

"It is a long story, my child, and one that you will be proud of. He was our king, and he was strong, proud and brave, and he loved you very much." Then she told me all about the war, the battle, how my father had been wounded, and how we had come to live with the humans. I couldn't resist one more question. "If my father has gone, then who will be our king?"

My mother sat silent for a moment, as if afraid to answer the question. "There are some things that we cannot know. We can see yesterday, we can see today but tomorrow is not ours, until it arrives." Then it was, at that moment, I was sure that a tear fell from her eye.

I walked back into the house, and with a heavy heart I climbed up onto the bed, nestled between the pillows and buried my tears there. Tears for a father I had never known, and for the fate that he had suffered. I wanted to know more, but for now this was all I could cope with. Tomorrow was another day. Tomorrow could wait.

*

"Princess, do you want to come for a walk on the beach with me?" Ma called to me as I was licking my breakfast bowl clean. "It's a beautiful morning, just right for a stroll."

She opened the gate and walked off down the pebble path towards the sea. I was a bit reluctant to go beyond the

19

steps, but a few of my cousins had decided that it would be fun to follow her. Ma had picked up an old piece of string that had been washed up on the shore, tied a bit of seaweed on the end and was dragging it along the sand as she walked. My cousins took to this like fish to the bait and chased after it.

I sat there watching for a while and then, with a little feeling of jealousy, I made my way down to join the others. Not to take part in the game, but to run on ahead, with my bell tinkling as I bounded along the water's edge, skipping and jumping over the small splashing waves as they rolled onto the sand. The fresh sea air and the warm sunshine were so invigorating. Everyone was having such fun and was so disappointed when the journey was over. The elders, however, scattered in their various positions along the beach, seemed glad when the last of us were safely home.

This became a daily routine for Ma and her "brood", as she called us. Except, of course, if it rained, or the weather was too rough. Every time we went out, the line seemed to get longer. More and more of the family joined in, even my mother and aunt took part. Once, some human tourists who had come to the seaside for the day had taken a few photographs of the spectacle. I suppose no one had ever seen such a sight before: twenty-four cats of various shapes and sizes, all in a line, following behind a human who is dragging a piece of string, is not something you see every day.

It was while on one of these walks that I noticed most of my family were female. There were only five males, one of them being my older brother. He was almost an adult now. Although he was big and strong, he had such calmness about him, and he was kind and gentle too. Ma had given him a name. She had called him Tigger, because he looked like a ginger tiger, but she added an extra G for his gentleness. I couldn't help wondering if he was like my father, and surely, being my father's son, that made him a prince.

His best friend was my cousin, who had been rescued from death's door by the humans a year or so ago. Although my cousin was a nice enough boy, he was a bit odd. He had squint eyes and whenever he sat still, his head would wobble as if he was nodding, so the humans named him Noddy, which, I have to say, I found quite amusing. The two of them, Tigger and Noddy, were always together, off chasing something or other. The other usually meant girls.

Although he and my brother were the best of friends, Noddy was also very fond of my two older sisters, Rose and Petal. It was easy to see why they had been given those names; they were truly beautiful, and the envy of all the other females. Rose was the friendly and outgoing one, while Petal was shy and subdued.

There were only three other males in our family, of which two were Noddy's younger brothers, from the latest of my aunt Coral's litter. Then there was one other boy, who seemed to belong to no one but nonetheless was part of the family. There was a suspicion that he was Petal's little boy, but no one knew for sure. He had been given the name Dinky, obviously because of his size.

Ma hadn't given everyone a name; it seemed that only the older members were given one. I guessed that the younger group of the family probably had to wait until they had grown, and she had found a name that suited their personality.

Whenever we finished our walk, Ma would count each of us as we climbed the steps and passed through the gate. She never took it for granted that everyone came back. Sometimes one or two would go off into the rocks to investigate and lose their way, or get left behind, but the gate was never shut until everyone had been accounted for.

*

Most evenings Ma and Danny would sit on the patio in their big blue wicker chairs, watching the sun set over the mountains on the other side of the bay. As the sky grew red on one side, the moon would rise on the other. One by one the stars would take their place in the night sky. I would lie on Ma's lap as she stroked me, while the rest of the family would drape themselves over the walls or furniture. We would sit there until the last of the pink sky had vanished and only the black of the night remained; then Ma and Danny would retire to bed, followed of course by me. The door closed behind us, leaving everyone else asleep on the patio furniture.

Except on the night of the full moon. I had witnessed the rituals of my family on such nights. One by one, the elders would slowly make their way to the water's edge, where they would gather and stare out to sea, as the moon made its journey across the sky. I was always curious about the reason for this strange happening.

A few weeks before my grandmother passed away, my curiosity overwhelmed me and, taking my fate into my own hands, I crept very quietly down to where they all sat. I hoped I would not be seen, since they had their backs to me, and that I might be able to hear what they were saying.

But I had forgotten about the bell on my collar, and before I even had time to sit on my chosen spot, my mother, hearing a tinkle, turned around. I caught my breath as our eyes met, but instead of chiding me, she called to me to come and join her. I crept slowly up to her and my grandmother, not quite sure of what I was letting myself into.

"There is no need to be afraid, my child," My mother's voice was reassuring, so I nestled beside her. She greeted me with a lick on my forehead and said, "The very fact that you are here, my child, tells us that you are ready."

I was a little nervous as to what was about to come, but at the same time I felt a sense of importance. Not only had I been accepted into this mysterious gathering, but I was also about to discover the mystery behind it. I looked up at the moon as it hung like a golden ball in the night sky, glistening on the almost motionless sea, and outlining our silhouettes as it sailed above. We sat there in silence for a while, as if waiting for the perfect moment.

My grandmother finally turned to me and said, "I am going to tell you a story, my child, and I want you to listen very carefully. We have watched you grow, and seen how your hunger to learn has put you apart from your siblings. You have the makings of a good leader, and one day you will make a perfect queen." She paused to collect her thoughts, before beginning her tale.

"Many, many moons ago..." my grandmother's voice was soft "...there was a land where the Sun was the Almighty God, and the humans who lived there were called the Sun Worshippers. They were a great and powerful people, who built many great cities and monuments in honour of their Sun God. Their wealth and knowledge were the envy of many great kings and emperors of the world, and since envy is the root of all evil, war was never far from their door."

Pausing again for a moment, she looked down at me. "Our ancestors held a very important place in this wondrous land. We had been bred to perfection, our very existence was to please the eye of the beholder, and we were given the status of Gods in our own right. Statues in our image were carved from great blocks of marble and gold, and were placed in their grand temples. Small carved figures of our image were hung on gold thread around the necks of the royals and other important families. There were laws passed that no harm should come to us, and we were free to roam in their palaces, temples and courtyards. We slept on the finest silk and woollen rugs and were fed only the freshest of food."

Again my grandmother paused and gave a small sigh before continuing. "To keep the threat of war from their land, the Sun Worshippers built many great ships, filled them with treasures and jewels, then sailed them to the emperors and kings of foreign and distant lands, as peace offerings. Among these treasures were many of our ancestors, chosen for their beauty as precious gifts.

"It was on one of these ships, on a night of the full moon, that our ancestors set sail on their fateful voyage. They came upon a storm at sea, and the raging waves and wind ripped the sails and tore the ship apart. All the treasure was lost but for a few of our ancestors, who were washed ashore, onto this land. They learned to survive and live on, but their lives were changed forever."

I sat there, soaking in the magic of the moment, listening to this beautiful yet sad story of our past, long, long ago. I couldn't help the feeling that my world had suddenly grown larger and brighter. As if a key had unlocked and opened a door to a wondrous place.

"I tell you these things, my child, as my mother and grandmother before told them to me, so that you may know your true history, and from where you truly came. The night of the full moon belongs to us. It is the Night of Reflection, a night when we should remember who we truly are."

*

That night I lay snuggled up in the pillows between Ma and Danny, unable to sleep, my mind full of images of my family's history. The Sun Worshippers with their palaces, riches, and sailing ships. All these images swirled around in my head like a fantasy. I dreamed of how different my family's life must have been, many years ago, in the land of the Sun God. In my mind, I walked through the temples and stood beside the great statues, which were carved in our image. I saw my mother sleeping on a silk rug, while my father sat proudly beside her.

Suddenly a piercing scream rang out from the patio, wrenching me back to the real world. I jumped down from the bed and ran to the window.

What I saw brought terror to my heart. My mother was being attacked by what looked like the enemy king, with my brother, sisters and aunt trying to defend her. The fight was furious and the terrifying screams ripped through my ears, striking panic into my very soul.

The flurry of writhing and screeching bodies escalated from the patio onto the cottage roof, and I lost sight of them. So, fearing for my mother and brother's lives, I jumped back onto the bed, and tried to wake Ma and Danny. "Wake up, wake up! Please wake up!" The clamour continued out on the roof and, together with my persistent pleas, it finally roused Danny from his sleep.

He rose and, realising that something was wrong, grabbed for his robe as he rushed to the patio, turning on the outside light as he did so. I was close at his heels, anxious to find out the fate of my family. As he opened the door, a few terrified young ones ran into the house, clearly in a very distraught state. The rest were hiding behind the flowerpots and wood pile.

Danny began shouting and banging on the roof with a stick, and almost immediately, the fighting stopped. Our enemy had come running down the roof, slipped, and was now clinging to the bamboo blind of the pagoda. Our eyes met for a fleeting moment, before he fell onto the sand below, and disappeared.

I turned to see my sisters and aunt descend from the roof. I ran over to ask if they were hurt, but was greeted by a chorus of hissing, telling me to stay away. They were obviously still fired up and wanted to be left alone, to assess their wounds for themselves. My mother and brother remained on the roof, and no amount of coaxing from Danny would bring them down. Deciding that the damage would best be left until the morning, he turned off the light and called to me. "Come on Princess!" I followed hesitantly, but snatched one last look for my mother before he closed the door. We climbed back into bed, but sleep would not come willingly to me.

*

The morning sun came streaming through the window, with the promise of a new day. I was the first out of bed, instead of being the last, as was my usual way. I went in search of my mother and much to my relief, I found her asleep on the patio table, with no visible wounds from the previous night's battle. Cautiously sniffing her body so as not to wake her, I looked for signs of damage and, finding only a few minor scratches, I settled down beside her.

A seagull squawked as it flew over the pagoda, waking my mother. She stretched her front legs, splayed her paws, baring her long sharp claws. She gave a large yawn, then closed her eyes and resumed her sleeping position.

"Mother, what happened last night?" I asked cautiously.

She sat up slowly, licked her paw and ran it along a scratch on her forehead. "Oh my child, it is only the burdens of being a queen and you are too young to understand."

"Is it to do with the war?" I pressed her.

Again she licked her paw and wiped her scratch. "For someone so young, you have a very inquiring mind, but I suppose it is a good thing, you will learn much. One day, my child, when you are a queen, all the knowledge that you have learned will stand you in good stead."

She told me that the enemy king was still determined to take her as his queen, and the land that belonged to my family. I remembered when she told me of my father's passing to the world in the sky, and how we no longer had a king, and that our future was in jeopardy. I also remembered looking into the enemy's eyes last night, and I knew he would never be swayed.

"Why can't my brother, who is a prince, take my father's place?" I asked.

My mother gave a little laugh. "While I agree that your brother would be a good king, I am afraid that it is not possible. It is our law that all princes who dream of being a king must go and conquer their own land and find their own queen. That is why there are not many males in our family, and now that your father has gone, I can only take a king from another land."

"So does this mean that you will surrender to the enemy king?" I asked, unable to hide the fear in my voice.

A look of uneasiness came over my mother's face, and she shifted uncomfortably. "I am not ready to make such decisions, not so soon after losing your father." She paused for a moment, looking out across the beach; then, turning to me, she spoke as if the words were too heavy to say. "The enemy king already has a queen, so not only would I have to surrender to him, but I would also have to surrender to her, or fight her for the right to be queen."

I shuddered at the fate of my mother, and as I looked down at my brother, who lay asleep on the floor below, I couldn't help wondering what the future held for him. His devotion to my mother was plain to see. He would fight in her wars, and fight to uphold all her decisions, but what would he do if she surrendered to a new king? What did the future hold in its hand for him? He was such a wonderful, kind spirit, with a truly gentle heart.

"Breakfast!" Ma called as she came onto the patio, carrying two large bowls. She set them down in their usual places, one bowl for the adults and one bowl for the young ones. Suddenly there was a hive of activity, as everyone scrambled to get at the food. "Come along, Princess," she called to me, so I jumped off the table and followed her to where my little pink bowl was waiting for me on the kitchen floor.

After eating the contents, I strolled across the patio, slid under the little wooden gate, and sat on the step to clean my whiskers and bask in the warm sunshine. This is where my story began. After everything that I had learned, and seen, I knew that I had made the right decision. I wanted to be with the humans, I wanted a safe, comfortable and happy life. Perhaps Ma and Danny were really Sun Worshippers, whose ancestors had also been washed ashore on that fateful night.

Were they different from the other humans? I couldn't really say. All I knew was that my mother chose these humans as a place of refuge in her time of need.

31

They seemed to understand who we were, and had done everything they could to help my family.

*

That afternoon, as I lay curled up on the sofa, with the smell of frying fish hanging in the air, I heard a knock on the front door. Ma went to answer it and I could hear her talking to someone. The tone of the conversation started off pleasantly enough, but soon rose to what sounded like a disagreement. The door slammed shut and she walked back into the kitchen.

"The cheek of it!" she shouted.

Danny rose from his chair, saying, "What was all that about?"

Ma banged about with some pots and pans, giving everyone a fright. She was clearly very upset about something. "Can you believe the nerve of some people?" she cried.

"Look, for goodness sake, will you tell me what's going on?" Danny insisted.

"Those new people, in their new houses, have formed a committee and signed a petition, saying that our cats have to go. They're saying that there are too many and not only is it a health risk, but it's not good for the image of the

32

beach. Either we have to get rid of them or they'll take action."

"What action?" asked Danny.

"Poison!" was Ma's reply.

I wasn't sure of exactly what was being said, but I knew something was wrong. I had never seen Ma this upset before; she was sobbing and Danny took her in his arms and tried to comfort her. "Don't worry, my love, we'll sort it out."

*

Over the next few days things were definitely being sorted out. In fact, it looked like we were being sorted out. First of all, three of my sisters were put into a basket and taken somewhere, and then some humans came and took the lovely Rose and little Dotty. Next to go was one and then two of my cousins. Large boxes started appearing, and all the ornaments and other things in the house started disappearing too.

My mother, aunt and the other members of our great family were beginning to panic. Even I was starting to feel very nervous. I didn't understand what was going on, but the family was getting smaller and it made me uneasy. Was I going to be next? Was I going to be given away? The thought must have been on everyone else's mind, because every time Ma went out onto the patio, they all scattered in different directions.

"I told you that humans couldn't be trusted!" my mother said, as I hid under a chair beside her. "Just when you think everything is fine, they prove you wrong."

I had certainly put all my trust in these humans. All my dreams were built around them, and I prayed with all my heart that I had not been wrong. My mother had never spoken of her reasons for distrusting humans. Perhaps they were justified and if ever there was a time to ask her, it had to be now.

"Mother, why is that you do not trust these humans, they have been so kind to us?"

"Oh my child, it is not that simple." she replied with a little hint of a sigh.

"What do you mean?" I urged.

Turning to lick my cheek she continued,"Yet another lesson for you to learn, my little one. You see, in this world there are three kinds of cats. There are the Feral kind, such as ourselves, who live their own lives as creatures of the wild. They have their own colonies and kingdoms, their own social patterns and have claimed their own territories, relying on their cunning, wit and hunting skills for survival.

"Then there are the Pets, they belong to the humans. Usually one or two Pets for any human family, and all their offspring are disposed of or given away, so that they have no family of their own. Their lives are spent in relative comfort and safety; they are fed and cared for, wanting for very little. In return, the humans are allowed to stroke them or, if for want of a better word, a little 'Petting'."

"But Mother...do we not live—" I tried to speak but she hushed me, and continued on her lesson.

"The third kind, are the Misfits, who are so called because they once belonged to humans, as Pets, but for some reason or another they were abandoned, outcast or lost. Their lives are lived eternally searching for a colony of Ferals that would accept them, or a human home to fit into. Their past comfort dulls their survival skills, so many perish, but those that survive live out the rest of their lives homeless, belonging nowhere."

"But Mother, we live with humans, are we not Pets?"

"No my love, we are not Pets. It is only by a twist of fate that we came to this place. Our land has grown smaller as the humans are claiming more for themselves, and it was only a matter of time that our lives and theirs would be affected. It is true that these humans have been kind to us, but not all humans are kind, we were extremely lucky. Does not the old fisherman's wife throw pails of water at us, do the human children not throw stones at us when they have nothing better to do? It is not that I do not trust these humans, but that I do not trust myself. I am a Feral queen and I can not allow myself to become accustomed to the human touch or rely on their care, it would only make things more difficult."

"Why not Mother, why not?"

"There are too many of us to live with one human family. I can not trust them to keep us all together, as a colony. That is the only way in which I do not trust these humans. Have they not already given away or taken some of your sisters and cousins? My family is disappearing before my very eyes and for the first time in my life, I am at a loss at what to do. I came here for refuge, to bring you into this world and to save our family, but now it seems there is no safe place left to go."

That night I climbed between the pillows, nestled up beside Ma and whispered a purr in her ear. "Please don't give me away or leave me behind, Ma." As I lay there, trying to sleep, I thought of how, only a few days ago, my life had been so perfect. How could things change so much, in so short a time? Was nothing in this life solid or worthy of trust?

*

The next morning, even though the sun was shining in the clear blue sky and the waves were gently lapping the shore, a feeling of dread was upon the house. A large car was parked in front of the cottage, and all the boxes containing Ma and Danny's belongings were packed into it. All except one, which stood empty by the door.

"Who's coming with us?" Danny asked.

"Everyone!" was Ma's reply.

I ran out onto the patio to tell my mother the good news. I was so excited; I thought that my heart would burst. "Mother, Mother, I knew they wouldn't abandon us! We are all going with the humans. They are taking all of us – all of us, Mother!"

She had been sitting on the floor in front of the gate, but as I spoke, she slid under it and began to walk away. "Mother?" I called after her. "Where are you going?"

She made her way down to the end of the pebble path that lead to the beach, and sat staring out across the blue sea. I came up and sat beside her. "I cannot go with the humans," she said, not looking at me.

"Why not, Mother?" I pleaded in disbelief.

She was silent for a moment, and then she spoke with a tone of sadness in her voice. "I cannot leave my land. It

37

is all I know. This is where my life is, here. I am the queen, and a queen can never desert her land, or her subjects."

"But, Mother, there will be no one here! Everyone is coming with us."

She turned to look at me, tears welling in her eyes. "I cannot stop those who wish to leave." I sat there watching her tears roll down her face and fall into the sand. "The time has come for our family to make a choice. I have done all I can to save us and keep our family together, but in the end, fate has played yet another hand in this life that is ours."

I stood up and walked around her. How could I make her see sense? "Mother, please, if you come with us, you will never have to starve, or endure all the hardships that you have in the past. You can leave all the wars and all your enemies behind."

"It is for that very reason that I must stay. Our family have been here for many generations, and yes, it is true, we have endured many hardships and fought many battles. If I leave, then it will all have been in vain, and your father will have given his life for nothing."

I knew it was no good to argue with her. I didn't want to leave her, but I didn't want to stay either. The life of a starving beggar was not how I wanted *my* life to be. I sat there motionless and defeated, staring at the sea, out over the horizon.

"Princess!" I could hear my name, somewhere away in the distance. Like a dream, or far away in another world. "Princess!" It came again.

I rose slowly, as if in a trance, and began walking back up the path. I tried desperately to turn and say, "Goodbye, Mother", but the words would not come out. They were trapped deep down in my chest somewhere. I reached the gate, slid under, and surrendered myself to Ma.

*

I don't remember too much of the next events. I was put in the box, along with the rest of my family, but it was dark and I could not tell who was in there with me. There seemed to be some kind of commotion going on, in and around the house, but I just sat feeling numb. After a while, the car started up and with a jolt it moved forward.

Our journey had begun.

We all held our breath for a moment. The strange feeling of motion, mixed with the fumes of the engine, was quite nauseating. Being a bit crowded in the box, every time the car went over a bump or turned a corner, we would fall over each other. In the end, any fear that anyone had been feeling was replaced with a sense of urgency to hang on to whatever or whoever they could.

39

The car lunged down the highway for a while, and then it turned north. After a bit more of the bouncing, bumping and turning, we began to climb. I guessed it was a mountain, because we just kept going up and up. The higher we went, the slower the car became, and the groaning of the strained engine grew louder and louder.

The further we climbed, the further I was getting from my mother. A picture of her sitting alone on the beach haunted me as I sat in the darkness of the box. My emotions were churning in my stomach. Guilt, excitement and fear, all mixed together. We kept on winding up and up the mountain, until I just couldn't believe that we could go any higher.

Suddenly, the car ground to a shuddering halt, then slowly turned a corner. I could feel the change in direction as it began making its way downwards, rattling and shaking, all the way. It must have been a dirt road, because we felt every bump and pothole, and smelt the dust in our nostrils. Much to everyone's relief, this part of the journey was shorter, and it wasn't long before the car had reached its final destination.

I heard Ma get out of the car, and the clink of metal as she opened a gate. Once Danny had driven the car through, again the clink as she closed it. When the engine was switched off, a strange silence rang in my ears, and I sat in the dark of the box, feeling very nervous of the world that awaited me outside.

*

It was a scorching hot late summer afternoon. The sun was still high in the cloudless sky, burning down on the parched dry earth. The light breeze, which gave no release from the intense heat of the day, lifted the dust and threw it into your eyes. I ran for shade underneath the car, while everyone else ran off in different directions to seek their own refuge.

"Water!" an old farmer called from a well near the house we had stopped outside. "Here, lots of water. Look!" he said as he splashed a handful over his face. "Come, drink!" He had turned on the tap and the water was gushing out into a large barrel. Ma and Danny took up the invitation, and were soon splashing their own faces and drinking handfuls of his water.

"You have many cats!" said the farmer, with astonishment in his voice.

"Yes, many," replied Ma hesitantly. We had been the first box to be lifted out of the car, and were now left to jump free. I wasn't entirely sure how many there were of us, I had a feeling that we weren't all here, but the farmer seemed taken aback. He was a sturdy little man, with a red smiley face and a straw hat.

After chatting for a while, Ma and Danny began unloading the car and the farmer went off to find an old tin. He filled it with water and brought it over to Ma, holding it in his hands like a peace offering. "Water, for the cats," he said. She smiled, thanked him and placed it under the car, where I was taking shelter.

I was so hot, tired and thirsty and I desperately wanted to drink, but my emotions were now just a knot in my stomach, and the fear of this unknown place kept me from moving. I just sat there watching and listening. It wasn't until everything had been taken out of the car, the farmer had climbed onto his mule and wandered off up the hill, and Ma and Danny had disappeared into the house, that I finally and cautiously took a drink.

That evening as the sun began to sink, taking its relentless heat with it, I crawled out from beneath the car. Looking around, I searched for something familiar, something that was home. The sea, with its blue water and rolling waves, had gone. The beach, with its soft golden sand, was gone. All I could see were mountains and trees. I sniffed the air for the smell of fish, but it too had gone.

What I did smell was the aroma of food being cooked. It was coming from inside the house, and it reminded me of how hungry I felt. So I followed my nose through the chaos and clutter of half unpacked boxes, all the way into the kitchen. "Hello, Princess!" greeted Ma as I walked in, and I knew that I was home.

*

The house was big and old, with an upstairs and a downstairs. It was very plain, with no pagoda or patio, and no plant pots or pretty flowers. There were a couple of outhouses and a stable. The house, which stood on a hill, was surrounded by trees, rocky outcrops, cliffs and mountains.

Ma had served dinner in two large bowls out on the forecourt, and the rest of my family were tucking into their meal. It was the first chance that I'd had to account for everyone since our arrival. I noticed immediately that my brother Tigger was missing. So too were my sister Petal, and my aunt Coral.

With my heart pounding, I ran around the house, calling their names as I sniffed all the boxes. I searched all the rooms then ran back outside to the car, but nothing. No matter where I looked or how hard I called, they were nowhere to be found.

Realising that they must have chosen to stay behind with my mother, my panic subsided. It was replaced with a feeling of relief and comfort. At least my mother was not alone. How foolish could I have been, to think that my brother would leave her? His devotion to her had no boundary, and was unbreakable. As were the bonds that held my sister and aunt to her side. They would never leave their queen, and if it was needed, they would lay down their lives for her.

I had paid a price to follow my dream, and just like the journey here, I too had climbed a mountain. I had turned my back on my mother and everything that she stood for. I had taken all the knowledge given to me, and used it to find my own happiness. I remembered the words she had once said to me: "Tomorrow is not yours until it arrives."

I knew that I would have to wait until the morning to see what it offered.

That night, I crawled into my favourite spot, between the pillows, beside Ma and Danny. We were in our new home, in a new place, and tomorrow I would start my new life. All the trauma of the day had left me exhausted and my emotions drained. Sleep settled over me like a soft blanket and I succumbed to its warmth, closed my eyes and dreamt of sailing ships and big fat moons.

*

I awoke the next morning to another beautiful sunny day. My heart was a lot lighter and I couldn't wait to find out what this new world had to offer. Ma had fed everyone, and my bowl was placed down for me as I entered the kitchen.

"Good morning, Princess!" greeted Ma with a cheerful smile. "We were just getting ready to go for a walk around the farm, so if you finish up your breakfast, we'll be off."

I was too excited to eat, but I managed a few mouthfuls and then trundled out into the sunshine. All the others had already begun their adventure of discovery. There was a large tree to the side of the house, and everyone was in it. Not having seen or climbed a tree before, it It was easy to spot the nervous ones by the way they clung to the trunk and branches; the more confident ones were on the higher branches, practising their balancing skills.

Ma came out and I followed her down to the gate. "Come on kittens!" she called and soon everyone was bounding along after her. We walked along an old dirt track that wound its way down to an olive grove. Excitement and curiosity were proving to be a hindrance, as every few minutes someone would go off to discover something or other, and then get lost or left behind.

Meow, meow, meow, the whole way, with Ma continually stopping to rescue somebody, and it must have got very confusing, because she kept having to count everyone. "One, two, three, four, five, six, seven, eight – oh, where's number nine? Who's not here?" Then she'd call, "Kitty, kitty!" until the last one was accounted for.

45

A walk in the countryside was definitely different from a walk on the beach. There were a lot more distractions, a lot more to see, and it was a whole new world. I was quite happy to see it all from either in front of or behind Ma's footsteps. I certainly wasn't going to get lost. Not out here in the wild.

I guess that was when Ma decided it was time to give everyone a name, or at least those who hadn't already been given one. Up until now she had only given the older ones a name, but half of them were no longer here. They were now a family that belonged to another land, in another time.

So over the course of the next few days, one by one, each of my cousins was given a name – probably chosen to reflect their colouring or nature, as Noddy's, Dinky's and mine had been. It didn't make the walks any less chaotic, but at least now Ma knew who was missing.

*

Of course, I missed my mother, but every day it got a little less painful. There was so much to learn and discover, or simply do. Things like climbing trees, smelling flowers, catching grasshoppers, and chasing mice and birds. Sitting in the shade of the tall grass or climbing the rocky slopes of the hills. Hollowed old trees and caves all needed to be

46

investigated. There was no highway or boundary to contain us, just wide-open countryside, and all the freedom we could wish for.

While we were off on our adventures, Ma and Danny busied themselves with the tasks of improving the house. Danny built a new kitchen, and put up a pagoda to shade the front of the house. Ma painted the walls inside, hung curtains and unpacked and placed all their belongings about the house. Next she began planting things around the pagoda, a lot of which had come from the cottage on the coast, including the pampas grass.

Danny also built a table and two seats, to go under the shade of the pagoda, and a bench to place in the sun beneath the kitchen window. All of which were soon occupied by the family, who were most grateful for somewhere to rest after their tiring days of adventure-seeking and discovery.

The last of the summer evenings were spent under the pagoda, where Ma and Danny would have their dinner and sip their glasses of wine, until the sun finally went down behind the mountain. We would sit around waiting for a tasty morsel or two, which, more often than not, came our way. I, of course, was the only one to be allowed to sit on the table, being that I was a Princess and had impeccable manners.

When the evening drew to a close, Ma and Danny

would retire to their bed, always making sure that the kitchen window was left open. I would follow, and nestle in my favourite place in the world, between the pillows. The rest of the family would either sit around outside, listening to the sounds of the night, or settle themselves on the sofa indoors.

On one particular night, Ma let me curl up in her arms. She hugged me warmly and asked, "Are you happy in your new home, my little Princess?" I gave a meow and a little wriggle, and licked her hand. "Oh good," she said and together we drifted off to sleep. I slipped into my dreams, feeling that my life was just how I had always wished it to be. Absolutely purr-fect.

Story Two

Warriors & Tigers

There were three of us: me (Tiga), my brother Niga, and my cousin Dinky. We were the bravest and strongest boys in the neighbourhood, and not to be trifled with. There wasn't a tree that we couldn't climb, a mouse we couldn't catch or, if need be, a fight we couldn't win. Every day was just one big adventure for us.

We grew up in the countryside, in the mountains, where there were plenty of trees, undergrowth and long grass, rocky cliffs that sprang waterfalls in the rainy season, and caves that were more often than not home to strange wild creatures.

We had marked out our own territory, and dared anyone to come within a few feet of our border. Occasionally, a stranger of our own kind would be caught sneaking around the perimeter, but we would soon see them off. Most of our days were spent, challenging each other's, battles of wit and courage. Of course it was always me who won. I was the best. I was afraid of nothing. My spirit was wild and free and my bravery untouchable.

One of our favourite pastimes was to chase and tease the girls. Especially the ones that fought back – they were dangerous. The three of us would chase one of them up a tree, until she had reached the highest and most unsafe branch, and then taunt her to our hearts content.

The rest of my family were girls, except for one other boy, but he wasn't much of a warrior. He was older than we were, but he had a wobbly head and squint eyes, which would be no good for hunting, or if he were ever in a fight.

So the three of us took it upon ourselves to become the Protectors of our family. We would guard them against any invaders. We were a force to be reckoned with. Niga and Dinky were the Dark Knights, I was the Golden King, and together we were the Warriors.

*

Our family had moved here, with the humans, several months ago. There were four boys, and five girls. None of us had any parents, so I suppose we were orphans. We were all quite young at the time, and my memory of where I came from is a bit vague. What I do remember is walking along some sand, near splashing water, and the long, dark and bumpy journey to get here.

The humans that we lived with were kind, and gave us everything we needed. We had a comfortable home, with plenty of food, and in the cold winter months, a nice warm fire. We were free to come and go as we pleased, but none of us would ever leave. It was our home, and all the land that surrounded it.

Sometimes we would all go for a walk with the humans, down country lanes or paths, through the trees and forest or even climbing the rocky slopes. You could always guarantee a good turn-out on one of these walks. Even if there were only one or two of the family at the outset, within a few minutes, the rest would make their way to join the party.

Being adventure-seekers, the Warriors always used these walks as a good opportunity to scout the layout of the land. We would sniff the ground for unknown or possible invaders, and in turn make our own mark, which was quite a handy thing, as the girls were always getting lost or left behind. Although we enjoyed our walks, we never forgot that we had to be on guard and ready for duty.

*

One evening, the three of us were keeping watch in the big old oak tree beside the house. It was our favourite vantage point, from which we could survey our borders. We each had our own marked branch, would take up position, and sit for hours discussing the things that warriors talk about.

51

My sister Dina had been so named because she was very good when it came to ball games, which we all played from time to time. If Dina got the ball, it was game over. No one, not even I, could get it from her. The humans gave her the name David, because she reminded them of some football player; but since she was a girl, it was changed to Davina. Then later, it was shortened to Dina.

She was a bit of a tomboy, was Dina, and had asked to join the Warriors, but I was having none of it. "We don't want girls in our gang," I had said. Although I was fond of her, and I knew that she wasn't afraid of anything, it wouldn't look good if we had a girl to back us up.

Anyway, that night, as we sat in our tree, Dina walked past. I called down to her, "Hey, Dina, where are you going?"

"None of your business!" she replied.

I sat up, had a little stretch and yawned. "Do you want us to come with you?" I asked teasingly.

"No thank you. I don't need any silly boys to watch after me!" she called over her shoulder, as she continued along the path.

"Please yourself!" I said, and resumed my comfortable position on my branch.

The night sky was dotted with stars, and I watched as one shot across the blackness, leaving a shimmering trail in its wake. "Wow, did you see that?" I called to the others.

"Yeah, it was a falling star," replied Niga. The air was still, and not a sound could be heard.

"Do you think it's an omen?" asked Dinky.

"No," I said. "Anyway, I'm not superstitious," I added, dispelling such notions. Deciding that all was well, with no sign of imminent danger, I called to the others, "Come on, boys; let's go get something to eat!"

Niga stood up and began scrambling down the tree. "Race you to the kitchen, first one gets the lot!" he called, as he headed towards the house. Dinky and I were right behind him, and the three of us jumped through the window and onto the kitchen floor at the same moment. To our disappointment, there was nothing in the biscuit bowl; someone had gotten there first.

This called for a plan of action and strategy, and with the latter being my middle name, I turned and said to the others, "Stand back and take heed!" So, leaving them where they were stationed, I turned and walked into the room where the humans were sitting looking at the big black box.

Ma and Danny, as we called them, had not noticed us come in through the window. To get their attention, I sprang onto Ma's lap and began to meow. She put her hand out to stroke me, saying, "Hello, Tiga!" I did the usual rubbing of my head on her hand, and gave another meow. This was repeated three more times, then I jumped down from her lap and made my way towards the kitchen, stopping in the doorway for one final meow.

Ma got up from the sofa and followed me into the kitchen. "Do you want some biscuits? Does my little Tiga want some biscuits?" she asked as she dug into a bag, and pulled out a handful. Dropping them into the empty bowl on the floor, she noticed the other two sitting in the half light. "I suppose you want some too?" she sighed, and put her hand back into the bag. "Three handfuls, for three hungry boys," she called as she went back to her seat on the sofa.

I knew that my plan was a winner, I had perfected it. Niga was useless, because once Ma started stroking him, he would get lost in the bliss of it. Dinky, on the other hand, hated being touched. He wouldn't let any human touch him, not even Ma.

We crunched on the biscuits, until the bowl was yet again empty, and then made our way into the sitting room. Niga and I took up our usual spot on the sofa between Ma

54

and Danny, and indulged ourselves in a bit of whisker-cleaning. Dinky had his usual perch on top of the big black box, usually with his tail hanging in the way of whatever Ma and Danny were trying to watch. The girls were curled up asleep in a mass of bodies on the armchair. All except for Dina, and the one who was asleep in the basket.

*

The next morning at breakfast, Ma noticed that there was one of us missing. "Who's not here?" she asked. We all looked at each other questioningly. Then it dawned on me. "Dina's not here!" I thought, with a slight panic in my heart. Ma must have realized it too, because she began calling her. "Dina! Dina!" But Dina didn't come.

I stopped eating and called to Niga and Dinky, "Come on, lads! Let's go find her!"

We charged off, with me leading the way, down to the path, where I had last seen Dina. We scoured the bushes and grass, went to all our secret hideaways and climbed to the top of the tallest trees, but could find nothing. "Where do you think she is?" asked Niga.

"Oh, she's probably playing a trick on us, and wants to enjoy making us look for her," I said, without showing too much concern. "If we stop looking for her, she'll probably get bored and come home." So we left it at that and went back to the house to wait.

When we arrived, Ma was in the vegetable patch, doing a bit of watering. Danny was digging a new row, ready for planting, and called for her to fetch the packet of seeds from the little shed at the end of the garden. It was a little brick building with no door, used for storing all the garden tools and things. Sometimes one or two of us would go in for a nap on the boxes, or on the pile of sacks.

We were just sitting in the morning sun, watching the goings on, when a cry came from within the shed. "Dina!" Ma shrieked, "Where have you been?"

I looked over at Niga and Dinky, grinned and smirked at them, "See, I told you so."

A second cry came from the shed. "Dina, what's wrong?" A pause, then: "Danny, come quickly. Dina's hurt!" He dropped his digging tool and rushed off to the shed. Realising that something was wrong, I ran up behind him and followed him into the shed. Dina was lying on the floor, with Ma kneeling down beside her.

"What's happened?" asked Danny.

"I'm not sure, it looks like she's been in some kind of fight," replied Ma, pointing to four gaping wounds on Dina's stomach.

"Yes, it looks like it was a fight with a rather large animal. Something with a large mouth has attacked her, probably a dog," said Danny.

I crept up to my sister and began sniffing for clues, "Who did this, Dina?" I asked. She lifted her head and tried to meow, but the blood in her mouth gurgled her words.

Again I asked, "Who did this, Dina?" but the whisper of her breath left her body and she fell back, motionless.

Ma lifted Dina's limp body into her arms and held her for a few minutes, cradling her as if she were a baby. "Oh, poor little Dina!" she kept crying.

*

Dina was buried beside a small orange tree in the orchard behind the house. Ma and Danny cried, and I blamed myself. I thought back to the previous night, and I knew that a star had truly fallen. Why hadn't I read the signs, why hadn't I protected her? All my guilt added to the pain of losing her, and I was left with a dark emptiness of self-doubt. I felt a failure as protector of my family.

I spent the next few days sitting alone, fighting with my emotions. Niga and Dinky must have realised that I needed the time to work things out, because they kept their distance. I had an inner battle to fight, between my pride and my conscience, and I had to do it alone.

Slowly, the doubt turned to anger, and then the anger turned to revenge. A burning fire replaced the coldness in my heart, and all I wanted to do was find this creature that had attacked my sister, and slay it! I wanted to destroy it, so that never again would my family suffer such a loss.

For the first time in my life, I felt the true meaning of the Warrior inside me. Up until now, it had all been a learning curve. It had all been a game. Perhaps I was no longer a boy, perhaps I had grown up. I had no father to compare myself to, no way of knowing, no one to ask. All I had was what I felt in my heart, and I came out of the darkness of self-pity like a raging tiger set free from his cage. I was ready to face my enemy.

*

I set off to find Niga and Dinky, and as it turned out, I didn't have far to look. They were sitting on the outcrop of rocks beside the house. "Hello fellow warriors, how are you both?" I asked as I jumped up to join them.

Niga turned to me and said, "I think it would be better if it was us asking you that question!"

"Yes, you're right, I'm sorry, but I had a few things to sort out," I replied.

"I think we all have," added Dinky.

We sat there for a while, in silence, each searching for the right words to say. Then Niga stood up and said the perfect words. "Dina proved that she was strong and brave. Not only did she fight for her life, but she escaped without being eaten. And even though she was mortally wounded, she made it home." His words stabbed pain into our hearts and together we vowed to avenge her.

For days we searched the land, looking for any strange and unusual smells or tracks. We had done this many times before, but this time it felt more focused. This was one of the most serious missions that we had ever undertaken. There was something out there, on our land, and we had to find it. All we knew about it was that it was large. This concerned us a little, but if Dina had faced up to the battle alone, then surely the three of us stood a better chance.

The recent rains had made our task more difficult, having washed away most of the freshest tracks. We did, however, come across what looked like a mud bath, in the olive grove to the north of our border. Some rather large creature had been rolling in an area of accumulated water, churning the ground into a pool of mud. The indentation of its body showed that it was definitely on the heavy side. Even the bristles of its hair could be seen in the dried mud.

The other point of interest was that we had caught sight of a black creature going into one of the caves on the far side of the cliffs at the back of the house. It looked like one of our kind, but was not large enough to be the enemy we were looking for. Although this creature was trespassing, we decided that we had more serious matters to deal with and would leave it alone. For now.

After four days of tracking and searching, we still had not found the enemy. We had set up a night watch, taking it in turns to guard the house and listen for anything unusual. It was while on my watch that I was stirred into action. I had been stationed on the arm of the sofa, my eyes closed and my ears straining for any sound.

I heard the thud of something landing on the tiled kitchen floor. "Was that one of us?" I thought to myself, and looked over to make sure everyone was accounted for. Satisfied that we were all here, I knew that it must be an enemy. The tiger inside me rose up and I lunged into the kitchen.

There was no time to waste; I had to destroy the creature. With the speed of a lightning bolt, I was upon its back, sinking my claws and teeth into its flesh; but the thick long coat of hair made it difficult for me to hang on, and my enemy managed to break free and leap back out of the kitchen window. With screaming cries of war, I went charging after it, following it into the garden shed, and attacking it with an uncontrollable vengeance.

Again it managed to break free and, now in fear of its life, it ran through the vegetable patch, jumped over the fence and bolted into the drain under the road. I was close on its tail, and no sooner had the creature stopped to catch its breath than I was lashing at it with my razor-sharp claws.

Suddenly, just for a single moment, I saw the creature for what it truly was. In my blind fury, I had not seen who I was attacking. My enemy was none other than a female of our kind. I had never seen one with such long hair before, but nonetheless, she was just a cat.

I took a step back, shocked and angry with myself, and screamed at her: "What are you doing on my land? What do you want in my house?" She did not answer but the look of utter terror in her eyes spoke a thousand words. "Get off my land!" I screamed. "And don't ever come back!"

Seizing her opportunity, she ran out of the tunnel, into the brush and up the hill, as fast as her legs could carry her. I came out just as my warriors were ready to go after the enemy. "No!" I shouted "Leave it be! It's not the one we want!"

*

Things had been a little tense around the house of late, so it came as a nice surprise when Ma and Danny announced

61

that we were going on a picnic. They had packed a basket and we were heading over to one of our favourite spots. It was a clearing on the edge of the hill that opened up to one of the best views of the mountains surrounding our house.

It was a fresh sunny day, with only a few puffs of cloud in the brilliant blue sky. Ma and Danny spread out a blanket on the grass and lay down to bask in the warm sunshine, while the rest of us went off to play or find some adventure. The game of the day was hide and seek. There were plenty of places to hide between the rocks, up the old olive trees and in the long grass.

There was always one girl who never took part in our games. She seemed lost in a world of her own, she was untouchable, and we all kept our distance from her. As a young boy, I had never really taken much notice of the girls; to me they were just someone to tease, but no one ever teased her. She would either stay close to Ma, or distance herself from the rest of us by sitting in a tree, and hissing at anyone who dared to come near.

The girls had all been given names. There was Monkey, a skinny wretch of a girl, who thought that everything was a tree, including Ma and Danny. Then there was Luvie, my remaining sister, who just loved to be loved and cuddled all the time. Marbles had been given her name because of her lovely marble-like colouring, and the last of the girls was probably named to mark the high esteem in which she held herself. Her name was Princess.

Having grown bored with our games, the Warriors and I took to enjoying the rest of the afternoon lying in the grass, while the girls went off to investigate the thicket on the other side. Except, of course, for Princess. She was off on her own, chasing a butterfly.

We sat there for a while, watching her. It was quite amusing to see her trying to capture her elusive prey. She would jump up, grasping at the air with her paws, only to find that it had fluttered away. We laughed among ourselves and dared each other to go and help her.

I was reluctant to take up the challenge at first. For some strange reason, I felt a little nervous of her. Watching her dancing about in the sunlight, her beauty and grace had stirred something inside me. I hadn't really noticed her like that before, and I didn't understand these new feelings.

"Go on Tiga, go and help the girl!" teased my Warriors. Not wanting to show my unease, I took a deep breath and headed over to where she was. Just as I reached her, she managed to capture her prize and was holding it between her paws. Noticing that it was not in fact a butterfly but a piece of silver paper, I stumbled over my words as I asked, "Hey, Princess...err, what have you caught?"

"It's a little piece of my father," she proclaimed.

Not sure if it was my nervousness or if I had heard her incorrectly, I muttered the first thing that came to mind. "It's a piece of tinsel, isn't it?"

The look of sheer delight at having captured her prize disappeared and was replaced with one of consternation. "No it is not. It is a piece of my father's wings," she insisted.

I was having a problem trying to understand. "What do mean?" I asked gently, so as not to upset her further.

"Do you see how it shimmers?" she asked as she held it closer to me.

I looked down at the glittering piece of tinsel. "Yes, I see."

Princess paused for a moment and then, with a hint of sadness in her voice, she said, "My father passed away, and now he flies on silver wings, in a place up in the sky. Sometimes, a little piece from his wings falls off and floats down to earth."

"How do you know this?" I asked, not quite sure of the sanity of this statement.

"My mother told me," she called as she slipped the piece between her lips and headed off towards the house.

Still bemused, I walked back to join the others. "What was all that about?" inquired Dinky.

"You don't want to know!" I replied and left it at that.

We spent the rest of the afternoon napping in the grass. As the sun dipped behind the mountain and the air cooled, Ma and Danny packed up their basket and we headed home.

*

That night, not long after all the lights had been turned out, a strange cry could be heard out in the hills. No one had ever heard the cry before. We all sat up with our ears pricked. Ma and Danny had heard it too, and were stirring in their bedroom above. I ran upstairs to find them both looking out of the window. The cry came again. The screeching howl sent shivers to your very soul.

"What on earth is that?" asked Ma in a half whisper.

"It sounds like a wild dog that's been crossed with a wild cat," said Danny.

I jumped onto the bed and gave a meow to show my discomfort. Ma sat down on the bed beside me and stroked me, saying, "Don't worry, Tiga, go and make sure that everyone is in the house. Danny will come down in a moment and close the kitchen window."

Without hesitation, I charged down the stairs to the sitting room. I called to Niga and Dinky to get everyone inside the house. Once all were present and correct, the three of us took our position on the window sill. The cry came several times, echoing round the hills and cutting through the still night air.

When Danny came down, we jumped back into the kitchen and he bolted the shutters. We were locked in and safe. "Don't worry, little fellows, no one's going to get you now," he said, walking back upstairs.

Dina had been on everyone's mind and it was Monkey who piped up and asked the question that we were all thinking. "Do you suppose it is the creature that attacked Dina?"

My Warriors and I looked at each other, raised our eyebrows and shrugged. "Maybe, Monkey, just maybe," I replied. "And if it is, we now know two things about it. One being that it is large, and the other being that it has a horrifying cry."

Niga spoke up, correcting me. "If it is the creature that we think it is, then there are three things that we know about it."

"What's the third?" I asked.

"It's dangerous!" said Niga.

*

As autumn slipped into winter, and we had slipped from boys into young adults, things began to change. Nothing had been seen or heard from the creature for a while, and our adventures had grown a little boring. We needed a new challenge, but didn't know what it was or where to look.

While the Warriors and I were out searching for our new challenge one chilly morning, we stumbled upon Noddy. He was sitting in the grass on the other side of the olive grove, with a girl. We had never seen her before, but I guessed that she was from a farm house further down the valley.

"Oh! Hello, Noddy," I said, a bit startled.

He never replied and I got the feeling that he didn't want us there. So the Warriors and I walked straight on past them, until we were out of sight. "Who do you suppose that was with Noddy?" asked Niga.

"I'm not sure," I said, shrugging.

"Shall we sneak back and see what they're up to?" challenged Dinky.

"Why not," I agreed, so we crept up through the grass, as close as we could without being seen.

"Oh no!" whispered Dinky as he peered through the tall yellow grass. "Noddy's kissing the girl!"

Niga and I snuck in for a closer look, and the three of us sat there in amazement, trying desperately to control our excitement and not let them hear our strained laughter. After a few minutes, not being able to contain ourselves any longer, we ran off into the woods.

"So that's what Noddy has been up to, all this time," said Dinky, still laughing.

"Yes, while we've been chasing girls up trees, he's been secretly kissing them!" declared Niga. Never having kissed a girl before, none of us knew what it was like, but it definitely looked like fun. And seeing the actual deed had gotten us all astir.

"Maybe it's what boys do when they're older?" suggested Dinky.

With all the excitement of the last few minutes, and too many new emotions racing through my body, I finally managed to pull my thoughts back together. "I think you're right, Dinky."

I looked over at Niga. The question on his mind could be seen in his eyes, but he said it anyway. "Do you think that we're old enough?"

Being that we were brave warriors and true adventure-seekers, I turned to him and said, "There's only one way to find out!"

*

Now that we were thinking of girls in a different way, a new plan of action was called for. We started spying on Noddy, watching his every move. We had never bothered too much about his whereabouts before. After all, what does a boy with a wobbly head and squint eyes get up to?

We learned that he usually slipped off after breakfast, sloped down a path at the back of the house, and made his way through the old olive grove, then through some thickets and down a road that lead to a small farm house. In the clearing around the house, we saw several cats lying in the shade of a large tree, and a couple of little ones playing on a log.

Noddy had walked up to the one that we recognised, licked her head and sat down beside her. The others didn't seem to mind him being there, which was quite puzzling. "They all seem to be girls," whispered Niga.

Summing up the situation, I guessed that he was right. "One thing's for sure, he walked into their territory without any sign of a guard. If you ask me, I think that this is all a bit odd, and we need to get the answers from Noddy himself."

The opportunity came my way a couple of days later. It was a rainy afternoon, everyone was huddled indoors

69

around the fireside, but Noddy was sat on the kitchen window sill. I climbed out and sat beside him. "Hello, Noddy," I said, "How come you're sitting out here?"

"Oh, I'm just waiting for the rain to stop," he replied with a hint of boredom in his voice.

"Did you want to go somewhere?" I asked, thinking that he probably wanted to go and see his girlfriend.

"Well yes, in fact I do have somewhere that I would like to be." He shifted his position slightly, wobbled his head and added, "You seem to be very interested in me at the moment. I've noticed you following me recently. What's it all about?"

I was a bit taken aback by this statement and wasn't quite sure what to say. It seemed that Noddy knew more than we thought he did. "Err, well it's not that we've been following you for any bad reason, Nod. It's just that, well, we saw you kissing a girl, the other day, and we were curious."

"Oh I see! It was like an awakening for you, wasn't it, and now you want to try it for yourselves?"

"Well, yes, you could say that" I replied clumsily.

He chuckled to himself and said, "So what do you want from me?"

I was beginning to feel embarrassed and managed to mutter the word "Advice?"

Noddy's head did another wobble and he turned to me. "Listen, Tiga, when the opportunity arrives, you'll know what to do."

"But how will I know when it arrives?"

"You'll know, believe me!"

We sat there in silence for a moment, while my brain ran through all the other questions that I wanted to ask him. As if he could read my mind, he suddenly looked up and said, "My girlfriend has got a few sisters!"

"What about Warriors?" I asked.

"None," he replied, jumping off the window sill and running off into the drizzling rain.

*

In the following weeks the Warriors and I went on a journey of a different kind. We put aside our hunger for war and discovered a passion for love. Noddy introduced us to the girls that lived at the farm house down the valley, and it wasn't long before we learned the art of kissing.

Niga and Dinky found two girls that they spent all of their time with, but for some reason, even though I liked one of the girls, I wasn't happy. At first, the excitement and experience was a lot of fun, but I soon felt that something was missing. I grew bored with the kissing and idle talk, and began finding excuses to avoid going down to the house.

I was walking up the path on my way home one day, when I spotted Princess sitting on a rock in the sunshine. She was alone, as always, lost in her thoughts and craziness. She was definitely an odd girl, but at least she was interesting. I decided to make a detour and, plucking up my courage, I strolled over to her.

"Hello, Princess," I greeted her as I approached. She turned to look at me, and I couldn't help catching my breath as my eyes took in her beauty. The sun shone on her pink coat, giving her a soft glow, and her golden eyes, defined even more by her lashes and whiskers, were set perfectly in her beautiful white face.

"Hello, Tiga," she whispered.

I started to say something, but she quickly hushed me. "Ssh," she said, holding her paw to her mouth. "There's a mouse hiding under this rock," she informed me. I crept carefully up beside her and peered over to have a look. We sat there in silence for a minute and then, sure enough, a little face, whiskers twitching, poked out from under the rock.

"Are you trying to catch it?" I whispered.

"No, silly, I am just watching it," she replied with a hint of irritation in her voice. I couldn't think of anything more boring to do, so I stood up, climbed down off the rock and began walking away. "Where are you going?" she called after me, forgetting to whisper.

"Oh, I'm going to take a walk over to the waterfall," I called back over my shoulder.

"Can I come with you?" she asked as she ran up behind me.

"Yes, if you want to," I answered, and continued along the trail. She sashayed a little way behind me, stopping every now and then to investigate or sniff something or other.

When we reached the waterfall, I sat on my favoured spot, on the bank beside the pool, and stared up at the towering cascade of water. "Isn't it wonderful!" she cried, revealing her utter delight at seeing such a marvel. "I love coming here, it always reminds me of where I came from."

"Funny that you should say that, it reminds me of somewhere too, but I'm not sure where."

"Don't you know, don't you remember?" she asked in disbelief.

I watched as she crept down to the water's edge and dipped her paw into the crystal clear pool. "No, I don't remember, I only have a feeling that I once walked on the edge of some splashing water."

"Well, I suppose you were still quite young when we moved here, and it was quite a while ago," she said with a sigh, as she stared at her reflection in the pool. "If your memory holds only the vaguest of clues, then your heart cannot grieve." She spoke softly, but I sensed a hidden pain in her voice.

I had never really been interested in trying to unfold the mysteries of the past or question my very being. This was my world, here, in this life. I was a Warrior, on a quest for my future, not my past. I had come here as a young boy, with nothing to remember except playing with my brother and cousins. I had grown up here, and learned all that I knew from this land. What need had I for a past that I did not know?

"Yes, you're right, the past is nothing to me, there are no painful memories," I said to her. "But it seems that you hold many memories?"

A look of sadness showed in her eyes, and I had a sudden urge to go over and kiss her, but my desire hung in the air as she turned away and ran up the path. "Princess!" I called after her. "Wait!"

But she had gone.

*

I tried to talk to her over the next few days, but she kept avoiding me. The more she ignored me, the more I wanted to talk to her. It was driving me crazy. Somehow, this beautiful, strange girl had gotten under my skin, and I couldn't shake her out.

I desperately wanted to win her heart, and thought of a thousand different ways to do it, but none of them seemed right. Then, as if by magic, I remembered the sheer delight on her face the day she had held a piece of her father's wings in her paw. Surely, if I could give her something that would make her that happy, then she would like me. So I went off on a search to find some of the elusive silver stuff.

It turned out to be more difficult than I had thought. Where do you find silver stuff in this vast countryside? I wandered around, searching here and there, up hills and down valleys. In the fields and orchards, in the long grass and between the craggy rocks, but it couldn't be found. I travelled for three days, crossing into unknown and dangerous territories, climbing through ravines, and dense forests, until I finally found what I was looking for.

I had been walking in an almond grove, far beyond our borders, when I caught a glimpse of something glistening in the fallen leaves that lay on the ground. My heart was racing faster than my legs could carry me, as I ran over to retrieve it. I scooped it up between my teeth as if it was the most valuable object in the world, and steadily made my long journey home.

"Where have you been, Tiga?" Ma was anxious to know as I came around the corner. She was busy sweeping the front terrace and, dropping her broom, she went to pick me up, but I avoided her and ran off into the house. There was only one girl I wanted to see, and I had to find her. I was tired and hungry, but I was on a mission and I wouldn't rest until I had delivered my precious gift.

I found her in the orange grove, a solitary little figure curled up asleep under a tree. I felt a warmth wrap around my heart the moment my eyes fell upon her. Still holding the piece of silver in my mouth, I walked softly over to her and whispered in her ear, "Princess, I have brought you something."

She awoke with a start, and I stood back as I dropped my gift before her. Staring at the piece of silver lying beside her, she gasped, and then her eyes looked up into mine. The surprise, the delight and the happiness that shone on her face was worth my endeavour. It was a moment that would stay with me forever.

"Tiga, where did you find it?" she cried in disbelief.

"I went to the ends of the earth to find it for you, Princess" I replied, my chest swelling with pride.

She leaned over and kissed me. "Oh thank you, Tiga, thank you!" And then, pausing for a moment, with a crease growing on her brow, she looked back into my eyes and asked, "Why, Tiga? Why did you bring me this?"

"Oh Princess, I just wanted to see the smile on your beautiful face," I replied, as the glow from her smile warmed my very soul.

*

We became closer after that day, spending most of our time together. I showed her all the land that the Warriors and I had claimed, and all the secret hideaways, and favourite look-outs. She, in turn, slowly opened up, and told me her amazing stories. Whether they were true or only a part of her wild imagination didn't really bother me. I loved to listen to her voice, and become lost in the tales that she told.

She had a world of knowledge inside her beautiful head and I found myself falling deeper and deeper into a dream of my own. "So, you are a true princess?" I asked her, one lazy spring afternoon, as we lay curled up together, staring up at the clouds floating along in the blue sky.

"Yes, I am," she replied.

It was the perfect moment to tell her what was on my mind.

"Princess?"

"Yes Tiga?"

"If I were to become a great and powerful king of all this land one day, would you be my queen?"

She gave a little chuckle. "Don't be silly, Tiga, that is a foolish notion!"

"A boy has a right to dream, does he not?" I said teasingly.

"And a dream is all it is, for I have no desire to be a queen."

"But, with all that you have learned, surely it would be wasted, were you not to put it to good use?" I urged.

Princess sat up, licked her paw, and stared out over the landscape, taking a moment before she spoke. "I made a decision a long time ago, Tiga. I want my life to be a simple one. I am just a pet, a human's pet, nothing more."

I sat up with a jolt, in shock and disbelief. "So you are prepared to throw it all away?"

She turned to look at me. "Tiga, don't be such a fool. I have told you everything, I have shared all my knowledge with you. It is now yours, and you can do with it as you wish."

"But you were born to be a queen, a beautiful and wise queen!" I argued

"Oh Tiga, how can I make you understand? I want only to live the way of my long ago ancestors, cherished and adored by humans. Fed tasty morsels in my own little bowl and a soft feathery cushion to lay on when I sleep. I would be useless as a wild cat, kingdoms and colonies belong to the Ferals."

"But Princess, we live with the humans, so you could have the best of both worlds. You could be a Pet and still be a ruler of a colony." I insisted.

"It would never work, Tiga. Already there are too many of us living with the humans, and when we have young, they will be given away, so there will be no colony to rule over anyway.

"Well, if you think about it, we were probably brought here, to this beautiful land, so that we might start a new and stronger colony. If it is as you said before, humans usually only have one or two Pets in any one family, then surely we should go and live in the woods? Perhaps Ma and Danny brought us here so that we could build a new life as the Ferals that we truly are?"

Tears welled in her eyes as she stared back at me and said, "I am sorry, Tiga, truly sorry!" She stood up, kissed my forehead and walked away, leaving me alone to stare at the empty sky.

With the spring came the birth of many new members to our family. Not only had the girls down the valley given birth, but so had Luvie, Marbles and Princess. It seemed that it wasn't only the boys who had found love through the months of winter.

So while the girls were busy with the task of looking after their young, the Warriors gathered to tell of their experiences and adventures. We had all changed, and I couldn't help noticing that Niga had lost a lot of weight. Noddy too was looking a bit rough, and was content to simply lie around, like a worn-out rug.

"So, Tiga, what have you been doing, we haven't seen much of you, lately?" asked Dinky.

I smiled and said, "Oh, this and that!", trying to avoid giving any details, but he caught the direction of my gaze and chuckled. "Ah, the Princess!"

Changing the subject quickly, I asked, "Has anyone seen Monkey?"

"No, I haven't," said Niga.

"Come to think of it, I haven't seen her for a while either," added Dinky.

Brushing my concern aside, I dismissed it as a matter of fact. "Oh, she's probably still off searching for love, poor thing!" And we all laughed.

80

A few days later, I decided that it was time for a mission to survey our land, as we had neglected our duties over the last few months. "Niga, do you want to come for a scout with me and Dinky?" I called over to him, as he lay on the chair under the pagoda.

"No, not today" he replied weakly.

"What's up?" I asked, walking up to him. He didn't look too good and I noticed strands of saliva hanging from his mouth.

I turned and ran back into the kitchen, where Ma was busy washing the dishes. Meowing several times and pacing to and from the door, I finally got the message through to her and she followed me. "What is it, Tiga?" she asked, wiping her hands on a cloth. I walked over and stood beside my brother.

She immediately saw the problem, and bent over to lift him from the chair. "You look ill, my darling. What's the matter?" She carried him into the house, calling for Danny.

After looking at him for a moment, Danny said, "I think he needs to go to the vet." They bundled him into a basket, put it into the car, drove up the mountain, and then disappeared. I sat for what seemed like hours, waiting at the gate until their return. Dinky came and sat with me for a while, but neither of us spoke a word.

That night, as Niga lay in his basket by the fire, I went over to him and asked, "What's happening to you, Niga?"

He lifted his head and looked at me with his large round eyes, so bright and full of life, and said, "I'm dying, Tiga."

I heard the words, but my mind refused to accept them. "What do mean? You can't die, you're a Warrior!" I said in disbelief.

He tried to sit up but there was very little strength in his body. "They say that I have a disease that cannot be cured," he said with a note of hopelessness.

"But you are the Dark Knight, a Warrior and a powerful fighter, Niga. Nothing can defeat you. Fight it, my brother," I demanded. "Remember the rule of all Warriors: life belongs to those who conquer their Fear."

He lay there with his bright eyes staring into mine,

"I am not afraid my brother, it is just that my strength is drained and I am too weak to fight."

"But you must not die Niga, I have so many plans for us. There is a great and wonderful future out there for the both of us."

He tried to wipe the saliva from his mouth before he spoke, "Oh, and what plans are these?"

"A kingdom; our own kingdom!" I replied, not hiding my eagerness to reveal all.

"A kingdom, what do you mean?"

"I mean a land that is ours, a land that has a king and a queen and its own colony."

"What has given you this idea, where has it come from?"

Realising that he knew nothing of the knowledge given to me by Princess, I thought that this was the time to tell him all about who he was. I knelt down beside his basket and began the tale of our ancestors, the sun worshipers, tall ships, seashores and big moons. I told him about the colony that lived on the beach, to whom we were born, our mother, our queen, our great king and the battle that sealed the great change in our lives. He lay mesmerised by this story and when I had told all that I could, we both sat staring into each other's eyes, for what seemed like a timeless moment.

Finally Niga spoke, "So where is our queen now?"

I thought for a minute before replying, "She is upstairs nursing my offspring."

Looking a little puzzled at my statement, "You mean Princess, don't you?"

"Yes!" I said, "But she does not want to be a queen. She has turned her back on her true destiny."

"So what will you do, will you find another queen?"

"Oh Niga, there is no one else for me. My heart is lost to her, but she will not have me, and I love her in vain."

"So what will you do, how will you build your kingdom?"

"With your help my bother." I urged.

Again he wiped the saliva from his mouth with his paw, before he spoke.

"Tiga, my brother…"

I hushed him before he could say anything, "You must rest my Niga, sleep, so that you can build your strength. This is a battle that you have to fight alone, but I will be here for you, if only to give you inner strength."

*

It took three weeks for Niga to die. For three weeks we all had to watch him grow thinner and weaker, until he was just skin and bone. He tried to come on the walks into the hills and countryside with the family, but he would lose his breath and collapse along the way, Ma would try to carry him, but he would have none of it. At meal times, she would

84

take his food to him, but he would defy his weakness and walk unsteadily over to join the rest of us.

He never lost his appetite to eat, and his eyes never lost their hunger for life; even at the very end, the fire still burned within. I know that he fought his illness with true bravery, as any fearless Warrior would, but the disease slowly consumed his body, eating away at his flesh and drinking the blood from his veins. Until, like a thief in the night, it stole his soul.

Ma and Danny did everything they could to make his days more comfortable, and when he finally passed, they wept and mourned him deeply. Ma held him in her arms and cried, "Goodbye my beautiful, big, strong and loving Niga. I will hold you in my memory forever."

As for me, I was feeling like there were cracks in all the walls that held my world together, and at any moment, they would come crumbling down around me. Losing my brother, my fellow Warrior, was like losing half of myself. It was as if a part of me had been stolen too. I felt unbalanced, and directionless. The simplicity of my youth had vanished, and I knew that I could never get it back. Nothing was making any sense anymore. For the first time in my life, I began to question my very reason for being.

A grave was dug for Niga beside my sister Dina, and the missing part of me was buried there with him. As they covered his body with earth, I managed a strangled meow. "Goodbye, my brother!" I choked and, unable to take the finality of it all, I turned and walked away.

The further I walked, the faster my legs began to move. By the time I had reached the house, I was almost running. I ran through the vegetable patch and up the hill, all the while running faster and faster, further and further. Over the hill and down into the forest. Then through an orchard, over a stream and up the craggy rock face. Running and running, without knowing where I was going. Until I finally collapsed what seemed a million miles away. I lay there, listening to the violent beating of my own heart. *Thump, thump, thump.* It was telling me that I was alive, and that my brother was dead.

*

I must have fallen asleep, because I was woken sharply by an awful screeching howl. I opened my eyes, and was unnerved to realise that I was not at home, and that night had fallen. For a moment I had no idea where I was, but then it all came flooding back, and I worked out my bearings. I honed my ears towards the howl, just as it rang out again.

"The creature!" I thought to myself, panic striking my heart. My next thought was to get to safety as fast as possible. I scrambled up a large old olive tree, and climbed as high as the branch would let me. I sat there, silent, with my nerves like electrically charged wires.

Again the howling screech came out of the darkness and I trained my eyes towards the sound. Suddenly I saw it, as it made its way through the orchard, almost invisible against the night. A shiver of utter fear came over my body in a wave, from the back of my neck it rippled down to the tip of my tail.

I had not felt this kind of fear before, and I was ashamed. "Warriors are afraid of nothing!" I kept telling myself, but I could not stop my body from trembling. I clung to the branch with my claws digging into its flesh, and my eyes focused on my enemy, hoping that he couldn't smell me, and that he would just go away.

I was still clinging to my branch long after the creature had gone. The sky had begun to turn pink with the morning sun before I slowly climbed down and, feeling tired, empty and defeated, I made my way home.

When I arrived, Ma was in the kitchen preparing breakfast. I jumped up onto the window sill and meowed. She came over and scooped me into her arms, obviously very concerned about me. "Where have you been, Tiga? You had me worried! That strange creature was about last night, I thought you might have been eaten!"

Ma was not the only one who was pleased that I had made it home. Normally a short hug was enough for me but on that day, I was quite happy to stay there and let her cuddle me for as long as possible. It felt so good and safe, and I was happy to put aside what was left of the Warrior, for a while, and just be a pet, a human's pet, her pet.

It was then that I realised what Princess had meant. I understood. That was the day that my dream slipped out of the window and was blown away by the wind.

Story Three

A Little Bit of Human Touch

I was born in the Sierra Nevada Mountains, in the chilly autumn before the snow came. My mother was of Turkish descent, a true beauty, with a thick long coat of silken hair and emerald green eyes. She once belonged to a wealthy human family, who had long since moved away, leaving her behind. There were many large houses in the neighbourhood, and she soon learned to fend for herself, begging food from the humans who lived there.

It must have been difficult for her, not having a voice. She was dumb, and could not meow, so I guess it was her beauty and her soft and gentle nature that won her favours. While we slept in the nest she made for us, under the protection of a thick leafy bush, she would set out to find food. Having two babies to suckle from her, it was not only her own hunger that she had to satisfy. As we grew older and her milk was not enough to satisfy us both, it became harder for her, and she would be gone for longer periods.

One cold wintry morning, my mother decided that it was time to move our family. Picking us up gently with her teeth, one by one, she carried us to one of the large houses where the humans lived. My brother and I had never seen a human before, but she must have felt it was safe to take us there. We were settled on a porch, next to a large wood pile. As she could not speak, we had to read my mother's actions to understand what she was trying to tell us. We guessed that the wood pile meant, "Hide in there". With that we darted between the logs, disappeared from sight, and waited. My mother sat there waiting too, her tail curled around her legs, staring silently up at a window.

After what seemed like ages, the window opened, and a human voice called out, "Hello pussycat, have you come for a bit of dinner? Are you hungry?" My mother stood up and did a little twirl in reply, then jumped onto the window sill and rubbed herself against the glass. The human disappeared for a few minutes, then came out onto the porch carrying a saucer of some nice-smelling brown stuff, and set it down in front of my mother, who did another twirl before tucking into her meal.

Although the human could not see us, we saw her, and were terrified. We were too frightened to come out of our hideout, so we stayed there until it was dark. I was the first to creep out from under the log pile. My mother was lying on the porch wall, the glow of the moon shining on her dark coat, and when I looked into her bright green eyes, I knew that it was safe. I was hungry so I walked over to the saucer of brown stuff, sniffed at it and, realising that my mother had only eaten half of the contents, I began to eat. I was soon joined by my brother, and together we licked the plate clean.

For the next few days this was the routine. Every evening my mother would sit on the porch, and every evening the human would give her a plate of food. My brother and I would always hide until the coast was clear. The only problem we had was that it was so boring having to hide all day. I wanted to play out in the crisp sunshine and go exploring. I realised that I had to get rid of my fear. So, summoning up all my courage, I ventured cautiously out into the unknown.

After climbing up and down the wood pile a couple of times, and chasing a wood louse or two, I found a rusty bottle top that made a tinkling sound when I pushed it across the stone floor. I was having such fun, and soon my brother crept out to see what was going on. He was always the more cautious one, alert, tense and ready for danger, and just sat there, his ears twitching. I tried to get him to join in the game but he was having none of it.

It was at this moment that the window opened, and a human face popped out. We both ran for cover, terrified. With our hair standing straight up from our bodies, and shaking with fear, we hid under the logs. The human voice called out, "John, there are two kittens out on the porch. Oh my God, the cat has brought her babies here!" Then another voice replied, "I told you not to feed that cat, you'll start a colony." Then the window closed. I was not sure why, but I felt that it was a mistake to let the humans see me. So I just stayed hidden under my log and tried to pretend that I wasn't really there.

That evening, the human came out on to the porch with a bigger bowl of nice smelling brown stuff, but instead of leaving it on the floor, she called to my brother and me, "Here kitty, here kitty, come and see what a lovely dinner I've got for you, here kitty!" After several attempts to coax us out and realising that we were not having any of it, she walked back into the house, leaving the plate behind. It wasn't until the night had grown dark, with only the sound of a few chirping crickets, that we came out to feed.

The following morning the human left food without calling to us. We waited until it felt safe to crawl out, looked round to see where our mother was, but she was nowhere to be found. Instead, there was a strange cage placed next to the plate of food. After sniffing it a few times, we decided that it was not of any danger, and tucked into our meal.

A flicker of movement, a shadow on the wall and suddenly I was grabbed from behind by my neck and thrust into the cage. The lid was slammed shut on my head.

My brother managed to escape to the wood pile, but the humans were after him. After a lot of commotion, hissing and screeching, he was tossed into the cage with me. I was in a complete state of shock, frozen fear clouding my mind, but I could see the damage that he had managed to inflict on the humans' arms and hands. He was a fighter, my brother, and that day he tasted his first blood.

*

I don't remember much of the next few hours, except that there was a strange sensation of moving, and it made me feel sick. In fact I did get sick, at least four times. My brother was making matters worse by trying to escape, clawing at the cage and meowing in a frenzy of fear and anger. I noticed another cage next to ours, a figure cowering in the half light inside. Could it be my mother? I just closed my eyes and prayed.

We finally stopped moving, and I could hear the humans talking. "This should be far enough. They won`t find their way back from here." Our cages were lifted up and carried a little distance, put down and the lids opened. Not sure of where we were, or what would happen next, we all just sat in the relative safety of our cages. After a few minutes, I saw my mother spring out from her cage and make a dash for some nearby brush. We took this as a signal, following close behind.

The humans left a large bowl of brown stuff under a big old tree, climbed into their nasty smelling moving machine and disappeared up over the hill, leaving the three of us hiding under a bush, in the middle of what felt like nowhere.

The night began to cover the sky with darkness, and I could feel the cold drops of rain on my back. We just sat there in silence. For some reason my mother did not want to move. As the rain set in, sensing my discomfort, she leaned over and began to lick my cheek. I nuzzled into her warm coat and, joined by my brother, we all huddled together and tried to sleep.

When I awoke the next morning, the rain had passed and the sun was shining through the last of the clouds. I crept out from under the brush to find my mother and brother tucking into the bowl of brown stuff under the tree. I walked over and joined in, and together we feasted until there was nothing left. With our tummies full, we sat in the long grass, watching my mother preen herself. She looked like a princess, so graceful and peaceful, without an apparent care in the world.

I had no idea where in the world we were, but I did know that it didn't really matter, as long as I was with my mother. She was so kind and always made me feel safe. I loved it best when she cleaned me. I could lie there for hours while she preened me and rid me of the odd flea or two. For a frightening moment the previous day, I'd thought that I had lost her.

We spent the next few days wandering around the hillside, sleeping in a cave or under a bush when night came. By the third day, I began to feel hungry and I wished my mother would find something for us to eat. My wish came true that night, when she slipped off while we were sleeping and returned with a mouse. To be honest, I didn't care much for mice, I preferred the brown stuff from the humans; but when you are hungry, anything is better than nothing.

We learned to go hunting with her during the dark nights, out in the wild. My brother was better at it than I was. I suppose he liked the challenge and the taste of blood, being a fighter and all that. I guess that I took after my mother, she did not like fighting. Love and peace were her thing; she was a gentle soul, with the beauty to match. Neither of us looked like her. My brother was beige coloured, with a chocolate face and tail, and bright blue eyes. Being slightly bigger than I was, he always got the upper hand, and was a bit of a bully. While I had my mother's large green eyes, I was just plain black. Well, not plain black, but a glossy black.

*

It was on a hunt one night that we came across a human house. A light was shining through the window and a delicious, hunger-stirring smell drifted out into the night air. This was not a large house like the one we had known, if only briefly, but smaller, less imposing. It was set amongst a small olive grove, beneath a rocky hill. There were many of our kind in the little courtyard. I had never seen any of our kind before. There were some sitting on the window sill, some on an old bench beside the window and others just sitting on the ground. They all seemed to be waiting for something.

Suddenly a little wooden door opened and a human came out, holding two of the biggest bowls of brown stuff that I had ever seen. Everyone gathered around the bowls and began tucking in. I remember licking my lips and wishing that I was one of those lucky ones. I looked up at my mother, but she made no move, so we just sat on the rock and watched. If there was one thing my mother had, it was plenty of patience. Time never bothered her.

It wasn't until the light went out and there was no movement in or around the house that she made her move. Walking very quietly and cautiously over the rocky ground, she made her way down to the courtyard in front of the house. She stopped for a moment, looking about her, and then slowly crept up to the bowls. There must have been a few morsels left and, after sniffing over them, she began eating. It was a sign that all was okay, so we made our way over to the bowl and joined in the clean-up. There wasn't much but it sure tasted good.

We soon settled into our new life and surroundings. Apart from the odd mouse or two, we fed on the leftover brown stuff, always careful not to be seen. My mother found a cave in the rocky outcrop above the house. Not only was it warm and dry, but it was a good vantage point from which to survey the house and surrounding land. Our days were spent sleeping most of the time, and our adventures in the night became our only activity. The dark of the night suited me though; being black, I was difficult to see.

*

One night while feeding on the leftovers, my mother noticed that the little kitchen window had been left open. The only light inside the house was coming from the glow of the fire in the hearth. Whether she was looking for more food or just being curious, I will never know. She jumped onto the window sill and slipped into the half light. My brother and I thought it best not to follow and sat waiting for her return.

A few moments later, a terrifying scream came from within the house. My instinct was to run and hide, but I froze where I sat. Judging from all the commotion, I could tell that it was a fight, and that my mother was in grave danger.

Suddenly she flew out of the window, followed by a large ginger male of our kind. He chased her into an outhouse and pounced on her, attacking her with terrible anger. I knew that the screams were not hers, she had no voice, but if I could have covered my ears, I would have. His attack on her seemed never-ending. I just wanted it to stop. The next thing I saw was my mother, bolting out of the shed and running for her life into the dark of the night, closely followed by her attacker.

I sat there shaking with uncontrollable fear. I turned to look for my brother, but he had gone. A few of the other members of the household had come to see what all the fuss was about, but all that was left was me. I wasn't sure if they could see me, since my coat made me difficult to detect in the dark, but no one took any notice of me. Then the light in the house went on, and I finally managed to move my legs, running as fast as I could, up the hill and into our cave. There was no one there, and I just sat in the black emptiness of the cave, trying to catch my breath, which was difficult with my heart pounding so hard in my chest.

Eventually, my trauma and fear subsided, and I lay there in the still of the night, listening for some footsteps that I knew. But only the sound of silence filled my ears. Then it came, a meow from the darkness, and my brother appeared. I was so glad to see him. We nudged noses, gave each other a lick on the head and then curled up together and waited for our mother to return.

*

That was the last time I ever saw my mother. I never knew what happened to her. She may have lost her life on that fateful night, or she may have been too afraid to return. She certainly would not have been able to call to us, as she had no voice. We waited for many days for her return, but she never came.

My life was so empty without her, and my tummy even emptier. It wasn't so bad for my brother; he could catch mice and things, he was really good at it. He had learned to hone his skills of attack. I watched him catch his prey, play with it, then finally eat it. I didn't really mind that he never shared his food with me, I was a brown stuff kind of boy anyway. I knew where to get it, and I knew how to get it – my mother had shown me that – but the fear inside me kept holding me back.

As I sat in the opening of the cave one evening, looking down on the little white house with the smoke rising from the chimney, I knew that, as it was growing darker, I was becoming more invisible. A surge of courage suddenly welled up inside of me, and I slowly made my way down the hill. When I reached the large rock beside the house, I did as my mother had done, and sat quietly and patiently, watching. There were a couple of the others around, and the big ginger one was on the window sill. I knew that he was not a force to reckon with, I had witnessed his vicious attack upon my mother. He was probably the guardian of the family and certainly didn't like strangers. So I just sat there in the dark shadows of the night, invisible, until all that was left in the courtyard were the bowls of leftovers. I made my move, cleaned out the bowls and slipped away into the night. While my brother had mastered his hunting skills, I too had mastered mine.

*

The long winter months soon slipped away, and the spring brought with it a sense of new life and growth. I was happy to be alive and I had certainly grown. My brother had grown too, and, I guessed, a lot stronger. I never saw much of him these days, he was always off on his travels. Sometimes I wondered if one day he would just not come back. Most of my days were spent basking in the warm sunshine, hidden in the tall grass, dreaming of a life in another place, another world. Or sometimes I would climb a tree and sit on a high branch, looking over the valley. I often wondered if my mother was out there, somewhere.

Although I was happy with my lot, I felt lonely and longed for company. To be honest, I wished that I could be like one of the others down at the little white house. I dreamed of sitting on the window sill and being fed tasty morsels. I dreamed of sleeping on a cushion beside the fire, and I even dared to dream of being stroked on the lap of the human. Not that I knew what it felt like, but the others seemed to enjoy it.

What I did know was that I was different from the others, in more ways than one. Not only was I an outcast, with no real home or family, but I had a fear living inside me, something they didn't seem to have. They showed no fear of humans, or much else, for that matter.

I spent many hours, in the dark of the night, hiding in the shadows, watching the happenings around the house. No one ever saw me, I was invisible – or so I had thought.

It was on one of these nights that I had an unusual experience. I was just sitting on my rock beside the house, waiting to make my move for a dinner of scraps, when this human voice spoke out of the dark. "Hello, what's your name?" I got such a fright. Who was she talking to? Not me, I was invisible. "I know you are there, I've been watching you for quite a while. You live up in the cave, don't you?"

I shifted on my feet, feeling uneasy. This human had spoken to me, she had clearly been aware of me for quite a while. Without realising, I was the hunter who had become the hunted. I was the silent observer who had become the silently observed. Panic struck my heart, but I decided not to run. The human was sitting in the dark, on the bench beside the window, which was a good enough distance from me. If I needed to, I could make my escape with relative ease.

"What`s your name, do you have a name?" I just sat there in silence. "Okay then, I`ll give you a name. Let`s see, how about Zeus?" Again I sat in silence. "Right, Zeus it is then." I had never had a name before. It gave me a sense of belonging, as if I was a part of something. Was I being invited to join the others? As much as I wanted to, I knew that it was not possible. I could never be one of them, never fit in. I jumped down off the rock and slinked out into the dark, weaving my way through the shadows of the trees.

I never did get any dinner that night. But I got a name.

*

After that night, I stayed away from the house, only going down to feed when my hunger forced me. I would go for days without eating. It wasn't just that I felt nervous of the human, but something else was happening to me. I was losing my appetite for food, and my strength was slipping away with each day that passed. It was as if something was eating me, eating my flesh, eating my body.

My brother had moved away, found a place of his own, and I was alone and afraid. Sometimes I thought that I could hear my name being called, stirring me from my unconsciousness, but I just lay there in the darkness of my cave.

Then one night, a strange thing happened. I could feel my life trying to rip itself from my body, when all of a sudden, the very fear that had kept me from trusting the human reared up like a powerful black shadow. Lifting my weak body onto my unsteady legs, it carried me out into the night. I found myself making my way down to the house, stumbling over the rocky slope, until eventually I crawled up onto the kitchen window sill. A gurgled meow came out of my mouth as I lay there trying to breathe.

A few moments later, I heard the human voice saying, "Zeus, what brings you here, a little food perhaps?" She must have realised that something was wrong, because she lifted me from the sill and carried me to the chair beside the fire. She put me down and scurried off, only to return with a bowl of brown stuff in her hand. She tried to get me to eat, but I just couldn`t manage it. Putting the bowl on the shelf above, she lifted me in her arms, sat down on the chair and lowered my trembling body onto her lap.

The warmth from the fire felt so good as I lay there helpless, while the human stroked me gently with her soft hands. With each stroke I could feel the fear falling away from my body, like the leaves from the trees in autumn, until all that was left was me. Just a boy, a lost boy. A wonderful feeling of peace soaked into my very soul. This was where I had always dreamed of being. At last I felt complete.

I fell asleep in her arms and lay there, in the warm glow of the fire, until it became a pile of embers. Slowly rising from her chair, the human lifted me gently and, placing me down onto the cushion, she kissed me on my head and whispered, "Goodnight, Zeus". Then she turned off the light and crept upstairs to her bed.

The dawn painted the sky with pink and gold as it hung over the valley that spring morning. The birds were beginning to twitter in the trees surrounding the little house. It was just as the sun popped over the hill, filling the world with light, that my life slipped away. As my soul was snatched from my body, I gave a gurgled meow, and with my last breath I managed to say "Thank you" to the human. And somehow, I knew that she heard me.

Story Four

A Place Called Heaven

"Luvie Loves Love" is what they called me, and it was true. You could love me, cuddle me, tickle me or stroke me all day long. I just loved being loved, and I loved to give love in return. If you happened to be a human, I would sit on your lap and kiss your cheek or nibble your ear, and if you were a cat, I would lick and clean you for as long as you would let me.

That's why becoming a mother was the most wonderful thing that could have happened to me. Having such cute and helpless little bundles of fur to nurture and suckle was the best feeling in the world. Not only was my heart bursting with the pride of having brought four perfect and healthy little ones into the world, but I was filled with the warmth of knowing that I had found my true love. The love that bonds a mother to her young. A Mother's Love.

I wasn't the only one in the household that had given birth in those last days of the spring. There were two other litters, one from Princess and one from Marbles. We were each given our own basket in our own corner of the house, in which to nurse our young in relative privacy.

Although I knew about the other litters, I had only one on my mind, and that was my own. There were three little girls and a little boy, who needed my undivided love and attention, and I certainly had more than enough to give. I was in another world, a world of pure happiness. I was in heaven.

*

I had been asleep while my young were feeding, when my brother Tiga came in to visit me. I hadn't seen him for a while and was a bit surprised when he popped his head into the basket. "Hello, Luvie!" he greeted. "How are things with you?"

Sitting up with difficulty and smiling broadly, I replied, "Oh Tiga, it's so good to see you. I am fine, we are all fine."

He sat down beside the basket and very cautiously sniffed at the bundles of fur inside. "Are you sure?" he asked.

"What do you mean?" I insisted.

"Well, nothing really. It's just that there seems to be a problem with Marbles. She isn't very well and I was just a bit concerned about you," he said, gazing at me questioningly.

"I'm fine, Tiga" I reassured him.

"That's okay then," he said as he stood up and walked away.

I lay back down, and resumed my comfortable nursing position, but my curiosity got the better of me, and I decided to go and investigate. So, making sure all my little ones were safe and asleep, I slipped out of the basket and made my way downstairs.

Marbles had given birth a few weeks before me and had been located a corner of the sitting room. She was sitting beside her basket, and three of her young were crawling about on the floor while the other two were asleep in the basket.

As soon as I laid eyes on her, I realised what Tiga meant. Her painfully thin body was made all the more obvious by her large stature. I tried desperately to hide my shock as I greeted her. "Hello, Marbles, I heard that you weren't too well, so I thought I'd come and see how you are?"

She stood up, walked over to retrieve a little ginger kitten that had ventured too far, picked it up gently between her teeth and returned it to the basket. "Thank you for your concern, Luvie, it is very kind of you."

Even though it was clear that she was ill, she still found the strength to care for her young. "Are you going to be alright?" I asked, fearful of her reply.

The look in her eyes told me the answer before she spoke. "Ma says that I have the same illness that took Niga from us. So, no, I don't think that I will be alright."

With my mind racing, full of images of my brother Niga's demise, I looked over at the little ones at her feet, and those asleep in the basket. "What about your babies?" I asked.

The tears welled in her eyes, and she spoke with such sadness that I felt a huge lump grow in my throat. "It is difficult to know. You see, not only are they too young to lose their mother, but they have suckled from me and my milk is probably tainted."

I choked back my own tears as I spoke. "I am so sorry, Marbles. I am truly sorry! If there is anything that I can do for you, I will gladly do it." I could no longer hold the flood of tears that had poured out of my heart and into my eyes.

"There is one thing that I would ask of you..." She paused for a moment and then, catching her breath, she continued. "If I should die, promise me that you will watch over my beautiful babies, and never let any harm come to them?"

With my heart almost breaking, I too gasped for breath as my throat tightened. "Of course I will do that for you," I said. "I promise to watch over them, as I do my own. I will love them and care for them, Marbles, but they will always be yours."

"Thank you, Luvie, you have put my mind at rest, and I will be eternally grateful to you. I can never repay you, except perhaps by wishing you the very best in your life. You truly deserve any happiness that comes your way. But I am tired now and I must rest, I must save my strength. Go back to your young ones, and I will see you tomorrow."

She crawled into her basket and nestled down with her little bundles of fur. I sat there for a moment, thinking of the cruelty of her fate, and how afraid she must have felt. I turned and, with a heavy heart, slowly made my way up the stairs.

As I climbed into my own basket, I prayed that nothing would ever happen to me. Feeling raw and vulnerable, I cuddled my babies closer than ever before and wept for Marbles.

*

Tomorrow never came for Marbles, but it certainly came for me. Ma burst into the room carrying a basket, "Luvie, I need your help!" she pleaded, as she placed it down beside me. "We have got to save Marbles' babies!"

It took a minute for me to gather my thoughts, and untangle myself from my suckling young, but before I could climb out of my basket, Ma had disappeared out of

109

the door. Panic gripped my heart and I ran down the stairs after her.

She was in the kitchen, scrambling about with a milk carton and some sort of tube. I glanced around to see where Marbles was, but she wasn't anywhere to be seen.

"Come on, Luvie, we've got work to do."

I followed Ma back up the stairs, to the room full of babies. When she had brought the other basket into the room, the bundles of fur were quiet, but now it was a squirming swell of meowing kittens. They were a little bigger than mine, but then they were a few weeks older.

Ma filled the tube with the warmed milk, lifted out one of the kittens, and then proceeded to feed it. Slowly and carefully, she dropped some milk into its mouth, and by the end of it all, the kitten was grabbing the tube and sucking for more. Once it had its fill, she placed it back in the basket and then repeated the process, until all five were satisfied.

I sat there, watching in amazement as all the feeding went on. The room had grown quiet again. I was just beginning to wonder what it was that Ma wanted me to do, when she turned to me and said, "There you are, Luvie, it's all yours now. Give them what you know best. Give them lots of love."

So there I was, my solitude and heaven, thrown into disarray. The arrival of five new kittens proved to be a bit daunting at first, but it wasn't long before things settled into a routine. For two weeks I rallied round licking, cleaning and nursing all my babies. Ma helped with the feeding and after the second week, the kittens were on solids and moved back downstairs.

Together, we had saved Marbles' babies.

*

My own young were growing so quickly and becoming more playful and adventurous. I was finding it difficult to keep them in the room and, reluctant to let them go, I was continually having to prevent them from venturing downstairs.

Ma said that I was too protective and that they were becoming too big to be cooped up in the room. She said I needed to let them play in the sunshine with the other kittens. I had enjoyed having little babies so much, I didn't really want them to grow up. I wanted them to stay small forever, but in the end I realised that I had to let go.

Once we were moved out into the big world, they seemed to need me less. Other than the occasional feed, my time was spent just lazing about. The older they grew, the further they grew away, and the more my longing grew to have more babies.

*

As the summer crept in, bringing with it the long warm nights, the older family members would sit on the bench below the kitchen window, while the young ones played in the garden. It was always a good time to catch up on the latest happenings and chat about all sorts of things.

One evening, as Tiga and I sat on the bench under the stars, he turned to me and said, "It's amazing how everything has changed."

"Mmm, yes I suppose it has," I replied, not quite sure where he was going with his statement.

"When we first came here, a year ago, there were nine of us, and now there are only five."

I thought for a minute before replying, "Well actually, there are fifteen now."

"Yes I know," he said, "but I'm talking about the older ones. If we have lost four in one year, who is to say that in another year, there won't be even fewer of us?"

I hadn't thought about it like that before and although he was right, I came to my own conclusion. "Having young is probably nature's way of replacing what it has lost."

Tiga took a minute to reply. "Well, I certainly don't want to be replaced."

"Mmm, yes I see what you mean, but at least the replacements will ensure that our family will continue to grow," I said

Tiga turned to look at me, "But how can our family grow Luvie, some of the kittens have already been given away, and more probably will follow?"

"Surely not all will be given away Tiga? Surely I will be able to keep some of them?"

He didn't answer my question, but sat staring out into the darkness of the night. I sensed that he was deep in thought, so I sat quietly waiting for him to speak.

"Luvie, do you ever think about where you were born?" He asked.

"No, not really. Probably in a birthing box somewhere."

Then he asked me a strange question, "Do you ever wonder what it would be like to live without the humans, live out in the wild?"

"What on earth are talking about? I couldnt possibly live in the wild, where would I have my babies? Under a bush full of creepies and snakes and things? No Tiga, I definitely do not think of living out in the wild."

A big smile grew over his face and he said, "Luvie you are so naive, but it makes you all the more sweeter for it."

Suddenly, as if his words had woken the devil in all his fury, a piercing scream echoed from behind the rocky outcrop beside the house. Someone was about to die, so without a second to spare, Tiga, Dinky and I charged blindly to the rescue. Moving with the speed of lightning, we found ourselves on the back of a huge hairy creature, our claws ripping into its flesh as it reared and twisted to free itself.

Our attack was furious, but our strength was no match for this powerful beast. Within a few moments, the creature had managed to shake us from its body, throwing us into the air like dead rabbits, before disappearing back into the night, leaving the three of us shaken and stunned.

By the time I had found my feet, Ma and Danny were outside with a torch, shining it across the rocks. "What on earth is going on?" called Danny.

I ran up to the house and began to look for the kittens. Realising what I was doing, Ma began to count them, making sure that everyone was there.

"We've got one missing!" she called to Danny, and together they went in search of the missing kitten. I knew that the creature hadn't got my baby, I'd seen it fall from the creature's jaws in all the confusion, but I was concerned for its injuries.

114

"I've found it, it's under the water tank!" yelled Danny, crawling under the wooden structure.

Once they had pulled the kitten from its refuge, and were determining any damage, I heard Ma say, "It's a little girl, one of Luvies'. She has some nasty teeth marks, but nothing too serious."

I breathed a sigh of relief, and walked over to see for myself. "You are a very lucky girl!" Danny told her. "I think that should be your name, that's what we'll call you, Lucky."

That night I lay beside my Lucky little girl. She was still in a state of shock from her ordeal, and I licked and comforted her until she finally relaxed and drifted off to sleep. Everyone else was asleep in a mass of breathing fur on the sofa. Except for Tiga and Dinky, who were keeping guard on the kitchen window sill.

I wanted to thank them for their help in saving my baby, so I slipped off to join them.

"How is she?" asked Tiga.

"She is fine," I replied, "but I wish to thank you both for what you did."

"That's okay," Tiga said, staring straight ahead, "I needed a good fight, haven't had one of those for a while."

"That's true!" said Dinky. "Things have been a bit quiet recently."

"You put up quite a fight yourself, Luvie, not bad for a girl!" praised Tiga.

"Why, thank you Tiga, but we don't want to be fighting that creature again in a hurry," I replied, a shiver running down my back. I already bore a nasty scar around my throat from a previous encounter with the creature. We all agreed, and climbed back through the window to join the rest of the family on the sofa.

*

Three of my kittens were given away. Little Lucky went to one human family and then two others were taken. I knew that I was powerless to do anything about it, but consoled myself in the knowledge that I would soon be having more. Two of Princess' litter went to a new home; one lived to be a few months old and then was taken by the illness.

I was sure that some of Marbles' kittens would have gone to new homes, but the fact that they had begun to show signs of illness was a problem. Ma and Danny had bundled them into the motor and disappeared over the hill several times. I had no idea where they went, but it must have been something to do with the illness.

By the time summer was coming to an end, we had lost four of Marbles' kittens. One by one, they were buried alongside their mother in the orange grove. Between Princess, Marbles and myself, we had given birth to thirteen kittens, but only three remained. Princess and I each had a daughter remaining, and there was a boy from Marbles.

Princess and I had never been friends. She had never let anyone get close to her, for that matter, except of course for Ma or perhaps Tiga. Since having her babies, she had grown more withdrawn than usual and I wanted to talk to her, but she would always hiss at me to stay away. Even her daughter was dealt the same treatment. Perhaps having her other young taken away had hurt her very deeply. Or perhaps there was something else on her mind. Whatever it was, she certainly was too complex for me to come to any conclusion. My life's a simple one and more rewarding, I told myself.

Not only did I fulfil my promise to Marbles by being a mother to her young, and doing the best I could, but I took it upon myself to care for Princess' daughter, as well as my own. I was always there to show the young how things were done, protect them from harm or give them a cuddle when that was all they wanted.

Tiga proved to be a good father figure; he had taken on the role with such ease that I was amazed. The big,

117

strong and powerful Tiga was just a big soft-hearted tom underneath his shining armour. He would always be on hand for any cleaning or cuddling that was needed, especially for the sick. He could change from being a warrior one day and then the next he could be a doting and loving parent figure. Since having so many young additions to our family, Tiga had taken on the role of Protector with much more vigour. Together we made a good team, loving and caring for the family, and just being happy to have a family around.

I knew that secretly, Tiga would have preferred that Princess was his team-mate, rather than me, his sister. And I knew too that he held deep, unfulfilled emotions for her in his heart, which I dared not speak to him about, for fear of opening unhealed wounds.

The only unfulfilled feeling I had now was waiting for the arrival of my new little bundles of fur. I could feel them moving inside my belly, telling me that they would soon be on their way. I would shortly be replacing some of those that were no longer with us. My basket was upstairs waiting for me, and soon I would be in that wonderful world of Life and glowing Love. That special place where only a mother with her newly born young can go. A place that I called Heaven.

Story Five

Darkness

"Where am I?"

The voice kept screaming inside my head. Everything was black, my fear was black, this place was black and even the smell smelt black. I was on my belly, my front legs fumbling nervously in one direction and then another, but the further I crawled, the more disorientated and frightened I became. "If only I could see!" I shouted at myself.

There were no stones to trip over and no trees to bump into. There was no grass or anything growing. Just a never-ending hard, flat and clueless surface and I was trying not to fall off the edge, if indeed there was one. It had a strange smell, a burnt oily smell, and my first thought was that it had something to do with the oil-smelling motor that humans used.

I was lost in a place where I was the only living thing, and it terrified me. I didn't know how I'd got there, and I didn't know how to get back. I tried calling, "Help me, please help me!", but no one heard me, no one came. I couldn't tell how long I had been out there, but it was definitely too long, and every second that passed left me feeling more frantic.

119

My heart was beating so hard, it made my head throb and I found it difficult to breathe. I could barely make out the whirring noise that was coming from somewhere in the distance. As the noise grew louder I realised that it was an approaching motor. I could feel the slight tremble of the ground beneath my feet, and my senses told me that I was in grave danger. In my blind panic, I tried desperately to find a place to hide in the empty darkness.

Suddenly the motor came to a screeching halt. It must have been only inches from where I was, because I could feel its heat on my face. I heard the door open and before I could gasp my breath, I was in Ma's arms, and she was crying, "Oh my god! Oh my god!"

I clung to her neck in sheer terror, screaming uncontrollably. I knew that I was safe, but I had endured so much fear and anxiety that I was in a state of shock. Ma just kept hugging me, saying, "It's okay, Bee Bee, it's okay. You're safe now."

When I finally calmed down, we walked home, with me still clinging to her neck for dear life. She had saved my life, and being in her arms was the safest place in the world.

"How did you get out of the garden, Bee Bee?" she asked me, but I couldn't tell her. It wasn't until we reached the house that she answered her own question. "Oh no! Someone has left the gate open. That's how you got out!"

You see, that's how it was for me, I lived in a dark world. You could see me, but I could not see you. I could smell you, I could touch you, and I could hear you, but I had no eyes, or at least I had eyes but they didn't let in any light. My world had boundaries and if I stepped out of those boundaries, I would be in unknown territory and possibly lost. Forever.

I had learned to live without light, and considered myself quite independent. I could do all the things that the other members of my family were able to do. In fact, I don't think they realised that I was blind, I hid it so well. To them, I was just slow, or too methodical.

Ma was the one who nursed me and bathed my eyes when the problem first became apparent, so she knew the truth. Although I am grateful for everything she did, I fought with her every time she tried to help me to do something. Even at such a young age, I knew that I had to learn to do things for myself.

There were times when I knew she was helping me, but she would do it in subtle ways. Like the time she realised that I couldn't join in a ball game, because I never knew which direction it had gone. So she got me a ball with a bell inside, or a thing with a fluffy tail that squeaked. If it made a noise I could find it, and once I had mastered my skills, I was almost as quick as everyone else.

When we went for walks on the farm, Ma would walk heavy-footed and drag a piece of string with a bell tied on the end. She would clap her hands whenever it looked like I was going the wrong way, or call out, "Come on, Bee Bee, catch up!" I was good at following sound, but if the wind was blowing things got difficult.

Long grass and small shrubs were a hindrance, but I just bounded over what I could, playing a game of hit and miss. I inevitably landed up in the middle of the brush or clump of grass, but I would carry on as if nothing unusual had happened. To any normal person it probably looked as if I liked to land in the middle of the brush.

Trees took a while longer to master, as I had to take care not to climb too high, just in case I fell. It was the unknown distance to the ground that frightened me. I always chose a tree that felt small; if I could get my arms around it, it was safe enough to climb.

The garden around the house was fenced off, especially for me, and I learned where my freedom ended. Except of course if the gate had been left open, and I unwittingly walked through. I didn't mind the restriction because the garden was large enough for me, and even so, I certainly didn't want to go any further and end up getting into unknown territory or lost. I relied on the fencing to tell me where I was.

Ma also kept all the furniture, in and around the house, in exactly the same place. She never moved anything, so I had a mental plan of the lay-out and I could get around without bumping into too many things. I had learned to be cautious; I would walk and not run, so as to limit the head-banging to just a soft knock.

My favourite piece of furniture was the sofa. Ma had moved the dinner table next to it, so that at her and Danny's dinner time, I could climb onto the arm of the sofa, sit on the edge and wave my paw in the air, asking for any titbits that she cared to give me. Ma and Danny always found this quite amusing. So the more they laughed, the more food I could get them to part with.

The staircase to the bedroom was the hardest thing for me to master. It wasn't too bad going up, but coming down proved very daunting. Not only did I have to judge the distance down to the next step, but it only had a wall on one side, and then on the other side, an empty, sheer drop onto the lower floor.

Being in the dark was bad enough, but emptiness was the worst. How do you measure emptiness, how far does emptiness go? I mean black is black, but black with nothing in it is very scary. If there was one thing that terrified me, that had to be it.

123

There was some light in my life. Well at least, it felt like light. My very life was my light, and it burned like a flame in my heart. I was a happy boy, and despite my dark world, I felt lucky to be alive. Ma was also a light in my life, I loved to be around her, and I had learned to trust her. She was my safety and I knew that she would protect me from any danger.

During the day (I knew it was day because of all the activity around the house and garden), I would follow the sound of Ma's footsteps. As soon as she came near, I would scurry up to her and do a little jump or two, with my tail standing straight up in the air. She would laugh and say, "Oh, you scared me, Bee Bee!" Or sometimes she would play a game – "Let's chase Bee Bee!" – and I would bound about the garden with Ma in hot pursuit.

At night, when everyone was settled on the big sofa, I would curl up on Ma or Danny's lap and go to sleep until they retired upstairs. I had learned how to climb onto the kitchen window sill, and some nights I would sit there, listening to the sounds of the night.

*

My own mother had died when I was very young. Her name was Marbles and soon after giving birth to me and my four siblings, she became ill and slowly slipped away from us.

124

Unfortunately, we all became ill, and one by one my siblings, too, slipped away. First to go was a brother, who was two months old, then a few weeks later one of my sisters. My remaining brother and sister lived to be four and six months old, before they were taken. Ma told me that they had all gone to join my mother in the land of spirits. I was the only one that survived, but the illness had left me without the use of my eyes. Ma tried desperately to save my eyes, but I hadn't made it easy for her, with my clawing and screaming.

Perhaps if I hadn't fought so hard, she might have saved my sight. But at least I know now that she tried.

*

One of my favourite things in life was to eat. I had such a keen sense of smell, I could always tell when there was any food about, and would always be the first to find it. I think that Ma had a soft spot for me because, if she was in the kitchen and I meowed, I more often than not got a tasty morsel. "Bee Bee, you're such a chubby little boy," she would say. "You really shouldn't eat so much!" But there was no stopping me when it came to food. That is probably how she noticed that something was not as it should have been.

I was about seven months old and a seemingly healthy boy. I had crept up the stairs one morning to have a cuddle in Ma and Danny's bed, as I sometimes did. Snuggling into the soft warmth of the covers was a good place to be, before the commotion of breakfast time.

Once Ma had trundled down to the kitchen, and the smell of coffee filled the air, I would wait for the clinking of our metal bowls before I made my move. I would feel my way to the edge of the bed, slip down the covers onto the floor, and then carefully make my way downstairs.

But on that particular day, I just stayed curled up on the bed. "Bee Bee, aren't you coming down for breakfast?" called Ma. I heard her, but I didn't feel hungry, so I stayed where I was. Again she called, and again I just lay there.

After a while she came upstairs, into the bedroom, "What's the matter, Bee Bee?" she asked as she sat down beside me. I gave a meow in reply and she stroked me. "Are you having an off day today, my little boy?" She snuggled me deeper into the covers and said, "Never you mind, have a sleep and you'll probably feel better later."

I never did feel better, and the next day I was put into a basket and driven up the hill, and down the other side. I had no idea where I was going, and I had never been in a motor before. I wasn't feeling too good in the first place, but the movement of the motor was making me feel even worse. I hated being in unknown territory and I grew frightened.

Ma must have known that I was afraid, because she began talking to me. "Bee Bee, you're so quiet. What a good boy you are! Don't worry, my love, you'll be all right." Her voice was soft and reassuring, but it didn't make me feel any better.

All through the journey Ma and Danny kept talking to each other. "We have to save him, Danny, he's the most beautiful, helpless little boy in the world," announced Ma in a tone that held a bit too much desperation for the likes of me.

"Don't worry, my love, we'll do whatever it takes," Danny replied with such certainty that even I believed him.

"Danny, we've come so far with him, I just couldn't bear to lose him now. He's become too important to me, I can't imagine being without him!" cried Ma, as Danny shifted the gearstick and the motor lunged forward.

"I know my dear, I know. I love him too."

I just lay there in my basket, in my dark world, hoping the journey would soon be over. And when it was, and we had reached our destination, I was whisked into a strange smelling building, where I was lifted out on to a cold metal surface. Ma was talking to someone who was prodding me all over my body with their cold hands.

I had no idea what was happening to me, or where I was, but it didn't feel good. Sensing my discomfort, Ma lifted me up and placed a cloth beneath me, and as I lay there, she kept stroking me, saying, "Don't worry, Beeb, it's going to be fine, you'll be okay."

A short while later, someone returned and, taking my front paw, stuck a very painful and sharp instrument into it. I gave out a cry, but Ma kept stroking me and telling me that it was all okay. "We need to do a test of his blood," said the person, "and you must be prepared for the worst."

Being in that place, lying on the cold flat metal table, reminded me of the day that I was lost. The same fear gripped me, but it was different, it smelt different, and this time Ma was with me. I had Ma to comfort me, and she would keep me safe.

The door opened and I heard the person walk back into the room. "It's not good news, I'm afraid."

Ma cleared her throat and asked, "What does that mean, what do you mean?"

There was a moment's silence before the other person spoke, "Well, it means that you have to make a very brave decision. The tests have proved positive, and the little fellow can only have one way to go. It's inevitable what the outcome will be, but the question is, when?"

"What are you saying?" cried Ma.

"He has the disease, and although we can prolong it for a short time with medication, he'll eventually die. If you choose to go this way, then his life will be difficult. He must never come into contact with any other cats, he must be isolated."

"You mean he'll have to live in a glass case?" whispered Ma in disbelief.

"You could say that, yes," replied the other person.

"But I can't do that, and even if it were possible, he would hate it!" Ma began to cry and I got very nervous.

"That's why I'll tell you the other option…" The person paused for a moment before continuing. "…the other option is to put him to sleep now." Ma burst into a sob, and I could feel her tears dripping onto me. "I'll leave you to think about it for a while," said the other person. I heard footsteps and a door closed.

Suddenly my world got darker, it was blacker than ever, and I tried desperately to find even just a flicker of light. I didn't want to be locked in a glass case for the rest of my life, and I certainly didn't want to be put into some kind of sleep.

My mind was racing around, trying to find an answer to the questions that Ma was asking me, and my heart was beating so loud that I had difficulty hearing her. "Oh, Bee Bee, my little Blind Boy, how can I make such an awful decision?" She was sobbing uncontrollably. "How can I do this, I don't have the strength?"

I didn't know what to do either. My fear was telling me to get up and run, but I was trapped in my darkness. There was no escape, I was lost. The dreaded feeling of emptiness, deep and bottomless, swept over me, and as it did so, Ma picked me up and held me in her arms. I lay there motionless, against her breast, listening to the beating of her heart, and I knew that there was no safer place in the world to be. The warm glow of love that came from her cradling arms was not enough to save me. There was no light brilliant enough to stop the darkness from swallowing me.

Whatever she decided, I knew that it would be with my wellbeing in mind. She would decide what was best for me. My trust in her had no boundary and I knew that she loved me dearly. Surrendering myself to her, I put my life in her hands. I tried to tell her this, but I had lost my voice; my lips moved, but nothing came out. All I could do was lie there, helpless, motionless.

When the time came, I summoned all my bravery and courage, lay down on the metal table and did as I was told. The sting from another sharp instrument caused me to flinch as it sank into my flesh. Ma stroked my body and kissed me on the head, saying, "I've chosen this way, my sweet, because I couldn't bear to watch you suffer the way all the others have done. If you're to go, then let it be swift." She lifted me into her arms and whispered in my ear, "I will love you forever, my lovely little Blind Boy."

As sleep dragged me down into the vast unknown emptiness, I closed my useless eyes for the last time. Perhaps I was slipping from this dark world, into another. Or perhaps I was going to join my mother, in a world full of glowing light and bright shining stars.

Story Six

Reflections

I looked out across the courtyard, into the soft light of the full moon as it cast silhouettes on the landscape. My eyes fell upon a solitary figure sitting alone on the wall beside the gate. I knew who it was and, picking up my courage, I jumped off the window sill and strolled cautiously over to her.

The twitch of her ears told me that she was aware of my approach. As I sprang up beside her, the flinching of her body sent out a clear message, that I wasn't welcome. I was prepared for the next sign, the hiss of disapproval, but it never came. So, moving slowly and carefully, I sat down, a little further along the wall.

She never did like anyone around her and, being a loner myself, I understood the nature of this. We had never really spoken to each other and I felt that now was the time. Since time was running out, there were things that needed to be said. No easy task, when the girl you want to talk to has locked herself behind a closed door, and any wrong word could send her even further away.

The moon had sailed through the wintry night sky and reached the top of the mountain before the silence between

132

us was broken. I had waited for the perfect moment to say the thought that was in my mind; and without turning to her, my eyes fixed on the big fat moon, I said, "There's something about the full moon that brings out the mood of reflection in me. Does it do the same for you, Princess?"

Her head turned and she shot a glance over to me, but said nothing. It wasn't much, but at least I had a response. I had guessed right; she thought she was the only one who knew about the Night of Reflection, and the ancient tales of our ancestry. I let the silence resume, before making my second attempt at getting her to talk to me. "Do you ever think about your childhood and where you came from?"

I could tell by her reply that she was uncomfortable with my questions, "Of course I do, doesn't everyone!"

I was going to have to try harder if I wanted her to open the door, so I dug a little deeper. "I knew your father. I was there on the night of the great battle."

Her head spun round, and she glared at me in disbelief. "You knew him, you were there?"

She had swung open the door, and all I had to do now was walk in.

"Of course I was there! We come from the same place, Princess. Only I was there before you, I was born a year before you."

133

A puzzled crease on her brow quickly disappeared as she spoke. "Oh yes, that's right. It's just that I hadn't thought of you knowing my father, everyone else was too young." I knew that what she meant to say was that she actually hadn't thought of me at all.

We spent the next few hours talking about the past and our lives by the sea. We were the only ones in our family besides Tiga who knew about our parents and our lives on the beach. I guessed that she probably told Tiga everything. Well almost everything. I still had a secret that I kept close to my heart, for fear of rejection. How could I tell Tiga that I was his older brother? Our mother was her aunt Coral, and I was the little kitten that the human had found dying at the mouth of the storm drain. I told her that I had lived with Ma and Danny for almost a year before she was born, and how I was the pampered little pet, and that it was the happiest time of my life.

"So what you are saying is that I stole your happiness?"

"No, don't you see, we have more in common than you would know. We came from the same place and both wanted the same thing." She looked a little uncomfortable at my remark, but I pressed on.

"Was it all worth it?" I asked.

"What do you mean, Noddy?" she asked in return.

"Well, I mean, was it worth trying to change your destiny?"

Taking a moment to gather her thoughts, she turned to me and said, "It depends, I suppose, on how you value 'worth'."

"All I know is that the best years of my life were not here, and I always wished that I could go back," I told her.

"Would it have been any better had you stayed on the beach?" she asked with a hint of reproach.

"At least I would have had my friends, if nothing else. Your brother and sisters were my friends, but here I have had no one. My life has been a lonely one. Even Ma has been too occupied with trying to save everyone else. I am not saying that life would have been easier, but at least it would have had more meaning."

"Yes, I think I know what you mean. My dream life never happened the way I had hoped it would." Her reply sounded so empty.

"What was your dream, Princess?" I asked.

"Oh, just to be a pampered little human pet."

"But isn't that what you are?" I said, reminding her of her status.

*

135

Ma had given me my own basket to sleep in, being as I was a loner and never slept with the others on the sofa. It was an old-fashioned cat basket in the shape of a tunnel, which, according to her, looked like a pea pod. So she aptly named it 'Nod's Pod'.

As I crawled into my pod later that night, my mind full of the conversation that I'd had with the Princess, I couldn't help feeling a little guilty. I had told her that our lives were carved from the same stone, and that she wasn't the only one who had lost a dream; but at least I had made peace with her, and in a way had said my goodbyes. I didn't want her to go without at least telling her that I understood who she was and what she had sacrificed.

I tried to sleep, but the calm soft breeze of the earlier night had grown into a howling wind. Shutters were banging, and windows and doors were creaking, as the wind swirled around the house. It was as if something was trying to get in, and I lay there in anticipation.

My thoughts went back to the question of "worth" and I wondered whether Princess' life had been worth it. Whether the sacrifices she had made were worth it. She had turned away from being a queen, twice. She had turned her back on her mother, and then on Tiga. Her only dream in life was to be Ma's Princess, Ma's pet.

All the other cats were a distraction from Ma's attentions, and all her privileges had to be fought for. She hated anyone eating out of her bowl, or sleeping on her bed, and the more kittens that were born, the more difficult it became for her. Her dream had slipped even further away, and she became more and more withdrawn. In the same way that it had been for me, when the old family moved onto the patio at the beach house, and my life was turned upside down.

My mind moved to Tiga, and what had happened to his dream. Unlike me, he was strong and brave, a Warrior, striving towards his own kingdom. He was the protector and guardian of the family, who had fought many different kinds of battles. His dream of being a great king had been crushed by the Princess he loved, and as salt to his gaping wound, even his manhood had been stripped from his body.

Luvie too had been denied her dream. There were no babies left for her to nurture and love, and no promise of more to come. All her young had been taken –given away, or eaten by the creature, though most had been taken by the disease. Except for one, the lovely little Smiley, a true beauty who grew to be just over a year old. Then one day, she vanished, just like Monkey, in a puff of wind. Probably stolen, or perhaps eaten by the creature – no one knew for sure. Never again would the house be full of little furry bundles and jingling toys. Was it all worth it for Luvie? I wondered. What was her worth now?

The wind had grown even stronger, and as it swirled through the groaning trees, I huddled deeper into my pod. I thought of the rest of the family, lying out there in the cold graveyard beside the orange grove. The disease had taken most of the family, until there were only the four of us left; and like the howling wind, it was beating at the window, trying to claim another victim.

Ma and Danny had done everything in their power to stop the disease as it spread from one member of the family to the next. No one knew from where it came, or who was carrying it, and there was a high probability that everyone had been exposed to the virus, and eventually all of us would perish. It was only a matter of time, and time was running out.

It wasn't the only thing that had run out. I had heard Ma and Danny talking about something called Money. I had no idea what it was, but it had something to do with their trying to stop the disease. Every time an ill member of the family had to be taken up the hill in the car, Ma would say that she needed more money. Sometimes, she would cry and say that she just didn't have any of the money stuff, and never went up the hill.

Tiga, Princess, Luvie and Smiley all had their breeding bits removed, so as to stop more births and stem the virus; so at least if they died, the illness would die with them. I was left intact, thankfully, but I guessed it was because Ma thought I would be the next to go, and I wasn't worth the money that she needed.

Sometimes death was swift, just a few days, and other times it was painfully slow, taking several weeks. I just prayed that when the disease finally got me, my death would come quickly, and Ma wouldn't need any money to take me up the hill.

I crept deeper into my pod, as the wind beat against the window above my head, trying with all its might to open it. The howling sent shivers in to my very bones. I closed my eyes, but the vision of an evil dark monster kept coming towards me, forcing me to open my eyes in fear. Sleep did not come easy, I had a demon to fight.

*

Over the next few days, I noticed a change in Princess' behaviour towards the rest of us. She would come and sit beside me, in silence, as I soaked up a bit of warm winter sun during the day, or she would snuggle up on the sofa with Tiga and Luvie in the evening, taking in the heat from the fire.

I guessed that our conversation the other night had made her realise that she wasn't the only cat in the world who had lost a dream, and that there was no longer any room for barriers of jealousy and regret. At first Tiga and Luvie weren't too sure of Princess' change of heart, but being the loving kind, they accepted her new friendly manner with gentle caution.

I, on the other hand, knew that I still had a few of my own barriers to destroy. Being a full grown male, I didn't feel the need for a cuddle with Tiga or Luvie. Especially as I had never let them or anyone else snuggle up to me. The big happy family snuggle wasn't my thing.

The occasional cuddle with Ma was more appealing. I had never forgotten how good it was, and now that there were so few of us left, I took the opportunity every now and again. She wasn't always eager to cuddle me, though – not that I could blame her. I was, after all, a bit of an eyesore. Since moving here, I had slipped into a depressive state of mind that grew worse as time went on. Having a wobbly head and squint eyes meant that everyone thought I was a bit odd, and they shied away from me. I was useless at hunting or fighting and was never invited to join in any adventures. I never wanted to be a great warrior or leader; a simple life was all I wanted. I missed my friends, and grew lonely.

The only one that showed any interest in me was a girl who lived down the valley, but there were always other males after her. This meant that I would have to hide until they had gone, for fear of any aggression. I wasn't a fighter and I definitely didn't like pain. I spent so much time alone, feeling that no one cared, and soon *I* began not to care. I stopped cleaning myself, and took on the look of an old tramp. Well, that's what Ma called me.

She tried to clean me on several occasions but I would have none of it, and eventually she left me where I wanted to be – alone. And that's where I have been for these last three years. Alone. I have sat and watched the demise of my family unfold before my very eyes, as if I was invisible, as if I wasn't there.

As the winter drew in, covering the sky in cloud and rain, I took the rare opportunity of a bit of crisp sunshine, to make my way down to a little clearing on the side of a small hill. Surrounded by tall grass and bushes, that kept the cold wind at bay, I snuggled down for a morning nap.

My solitude was suddenly interrupted by the appearance of Princess. Her illness had begun to show and her beauty was only a shadow of its former self. She was looking more delicate than was usual.

"Hello Noddy!" she greeted, as she walked over to where I lay.

"Oh. Hello Princess!" I said without hiding my surprise.

"Am I disturbing you?"

"Oh…um…no! Not at all"

She sat down beside me and I waited for her to speak. I felt sure that she had something to tell me, why else was she here?

"What is it Princess, you seem troubled?"

"No Noddy quite the opposite. In fact I think that I have found the answer."

"The answer? Answer to what?" I asked as I sat up and wobbled my head.

"Well… the answer to your question of 'Worth'. I mean was it worth Ma saving your life that day? Was it worth her trying to save all of us? Was it worth her making her own sacrifices to bring us here, to this beautiful place? There are so many questions of 'Worth' but I would answer 'YES' to all of them."

"That may well be Princess, but I loved my life; I loved my friends, I loved the beach, and I loved fish." I insisted

"Yes, I know, and Luvie loved having little bundles of fur and wanted to be a mother forever. Tiga wanted his own kingdom with me as his queen, and I wanted Ma all to

142

myself. None of our dreams came true so does that mean our lives are not worth living, that we are worthless? The truth is we were all given a perfect opportunity to be happy, but no one was prepared for what happened. No one could foresee the future."

Now my head was really wobbling, "Why are you telling me all this?" I asked in exasperation.

"Because I am trying to tell you that there is no point in looking back and that no one is to blame. We are the result of two worlds colliding. One being the Feral cat world and the other the Human world. Our parents were driven by desperation, and the humans moving into the little house by the sea, brought about the collision."

"But how does that answer the question of worth?" I asked, trying to understand.

"Don't you see? Life is worth it! Just being alive, even for a short while is worth it. Life is a gift and we should cherish every moment."

I sat there for a long while after she had gone, thinking of all she had said, knowing that she herself was dying.

For some strange reason my eyes filled with tears and I began to cry. I lay there in my snug little spot, hidden by the grass and bushes, and sobbed. It was like I was crying for the world. Uncontrolled waves of sobbing shook my body, as thoughts of my life and all my family swam around in my head. I wanted so much to think that my life was worth living, but everything seemed so black.

*

It had been the coldest winter I had ever known, and it added a dusting of snow to the mountainside. With the approach of Christmas, Ma and Danny were delighted by the prospect of more snow on the day. A tree with coloured lights had been placed by the front door, and the fire burned red in the hearth.

Princess lay on a cushion beside the fire, warming her frail body. Every time Ma went to place a log in the burning embers, Princess would cry to her, "Meow!"

"What is it, my little one, what do you want?" Ma would ask.

"Please hold me, Ma," came her reply.

Lifting Princess into her arms, Ma spoke softly, "Oh my little one! You're so fragile, I'm afraid I might break you." She would cradle Princess in her arms until the fire needed another log, and then gently place her back on to her cushion.

Tiga, taking his opportunity between cuddles, jumped from the sofa and went to sit beside her. Leaning over, he gently began to lick her forehead, and I knew this would be his last moment to be with his Princess.

"Princess, I have a little poem that I would like to share with you," he said.

"A poem?" she asked with shaky surprise.

"Yes, I found the words floating around in my head, and I wanted to tell them to you." He looked a little uncomfortable, and Luvie and I leaned in closer so that we could hear.

Tiga cleared his throat before he spoke:

> "You are my world, you are my light
> My sun, my moon and my stars;
> And when your soul takes it flight
> My heart will be left with scars.
> You are my love, and my dreams,
> You are all that I ever held dear;
> My heart is torn at the seams
> And my eyes, they shed a tear.
> I will never forget you, my love,
> So send me little pieces of silver
> On the wings of a heavenly dove
> that I may always hold you near."

The room fell silent for a moment, as we waited for Princess' response. Her frail body rose from the cushion as she sat up. The glow from the flames in the fireplace put a sparkle in her eyes, and the look of sheer delight on her face was plain to see, "Oh Tiga, that was beautiful! Thank you."

Tiga sat back, looking slightly self-conscious. "That wasn't easy for me, I'll have you know, but it was worth it, just to see your smile!" he said, beaming back at her.

There it was again, that word: "worth". No matter how much pain or suffering Tiga had endured, it was all worth it, to make the one he loved smile – even if only for a moment.

*

That night, as I lay huddled in my pod and the snow fell gently on the ground, Princess slipped out of our lives. She wasn't going to be home for Christmas, and I had lost the possibility of a friend and someone who knew who I was. But it was Tiga who had lost his everything. She was his queen, the queen of all his dreams and the queen of his heart. Even his great and all powerful love was no match for the evil force that would take her away.

The tears in her Ma's eyes told me that Princess' life and sacrifices had definitely been worth it. She had been dearly loved. She was Ma's little Princess, and I knew that she would be sorely missed, and never ever forgotten.

A little grave was dug in the soft earth just below the vegetable patch, and a young olive tree planted to mark the spot where she lay.

As for me, well, I still had to decide whether my life was worth it. The way I saw it, I had come full circle. I had gone from a scruffy, dying and unwanted little kitten, to a scruffy, dying and lonely adult. The bit in between had given me a few brief moments of happiness, but not enough to make it all worth it.

Perhaps my destiny was to die on the beach, at the mouth of the storm drain, that fateful day. Perhaps I wasn't meant to be here, after all. If it hadn't been for me, probably none of the events that followed would have happened. Life on the beach would have gone on as it should have. In truth, the humans had tried to change our destiny, but as fate would have it, a cruel hand had been dealt. I thought of everything that Princess had said to me and I knew she was right. My self pity had eaten away all my sense of hope and happiness. I had spent these last few years looking back at yesterday, but I, unlike her, still had a tomorrow. Was that her parting gift, I wondered?

147

A few weeks after the Princess passed away, Ma announced that we would be moving to a new house further down the mountain. She said that there were too many memories and graves, and that it was time to make a fresh start. The contents of the house were slowly dismantled and packed into boxes. The plants were uprooted and potted. I sat and watched as my home and my life slowly disappeared. On moving day, Tiga and Luvie were put into their carrying basket.

Ma came to look for me, but I was hiding in the orange grove. She called and called, but I pretended not to hear her. Realising that she would not leave without me, I knew that I would have to face her, and tell her that I didn't want to go. So, making sure that I was a fair distance away, I made my appearance.

"Noddy, where have you been? We're off now, come along," she said with a hint of irritation.

For the first time in my life, I did not obey her call. Instead I just stood there and meowed, "I am not going with you."

The look on her face told me that she couldn't quite grasp what I had just said. "What do you mean, Noddy? You must come with us!"

I wasn't going to try to explain my reasons to her; she would only make it worse by trying to talk me out of it.

Turning and running a few trees further away, I heard her call after me, "Noddy! Noddy!"

When I reached the big old oak tree, I hesitated, summoning a little more courage. Then, turning around for the last time, I uttered a strangled meow. "Goodbye, Ma," I choked. Not waiting to hear her reply, I headed off along the path and disappeared down into the valley; where I knew my tomorrow was waiting.

The End